# R4:14

## BEYOND TIME TRILOGY

### NOW-OWN-WON

## W. A. VEGA

• • •

Global Publishing Group LLC/Believer Books

BELIEVER BOOKS

Scripture references are generally taken from the New King James and the Complete Jewish Study Bible Versions.

Printed in the United States of America

First trade edition

ISBN  978-1-954804-34-0

# DEDICATION

This fictional work is dedicated to those with eyes to see, ears to hear, and hearts to imagine all that God has prepared for those who love Him. To the sons of God who are being revealed, in this time, this season and this place.

I thank my Lord, my God, who gave the mandate to:

*"Write the vision*
*And make it plain on tablets,*
*That he may run who reads it.*
*For the vision is yet for an appointed time;*
*But at the end it will speak, and it will not lie.*
*Though it tarries, wait for it;*
*Because it will surely come,*
*It will not tarry.*
*Behold the proud,*
*His soul is not upright in him;*
*But the just shall live by his faith."*
(Habakkuk 2: 2 – 4)

"….And who knows but that you have come to
your royal position
**for such a time as this**."

*(Esther 4:14)*

*A letter from Heaven for such a time as this:*

*Date: Today*

*My Beloved,*

*How could I ever forget you when you have been with Me since the foundation of the world? You are forever part of me. I sealed our relationship when I allowed My Son to die on the cross. Now you are in me because He is in you. My Spirit dwells in you and I Am with you always.*

*My precious child, let me shout on the rooftop of your heart that I will never, ever, no, not ever, leave you, forsake you or deny you, no matter what. I will never abandon or reject you because you are a vital part of me. I have sworn this by Myself, and there is none greater to swear by, that I Am committed to be with you always.*

*Believe my tears as they roll down my face and my heart as it exploded in pieces, when I rejected My own Son, My only Son, all to secure relationship with you forever. Beloved, if I am willing to do this, please know that there is nothing, absolutely nothing that could ever separate you from My love.*

*There is nothing that you could do to prevent My total and complete love for you. Little one, above all, I want you to feel the security of My love and presence in your life, now and forever. Just look to the cross*

*Forever in love with you...*

*Your Heavenly Father,*
*Abba*

*(John 15; Hebrews 14; Matthew 28; Romans 8)*

*(Excerpt from "Mi Cara ~ Letters From Heaven for such a time as this. W.A.Vega, Copyright 2015)*

• • •

# PART ONE

# INTRODUCTION

# NOW

It was a season where fear ruled and reigned, internally and externally. Lurking in plain sight, he was the undercurrent dictating thought, word and deed. No respecter of persons, this unseen, invasive and pervasive predator, roamed like a roaring lion, seeking whom he may devour. (1Peter 5:6) His one and only objective was to steal, kill and destroy. (John 10:10) Targeting the weak and strong, the rich and poor, the young and old, the wise and foolish, he relentlessly pursued every heart hoping it would buckle in uncontested surrender.

There was no other season in history when the human heart was as vulnerable to every whimper of threat. Everyone was viewed as a potential enemy. Notwithstanding, without recognizing the strategy of the enemy within, the masses focused on perceived external adversaries. In spite of their best efforts, safety and security became an elusive dream of former times. In high demand and bought at any price, maximum security was the one assurance ruthlessly pursued by individuals, families, cities, countries, continents and the entire world.

Thinking they were protecting themselves from an external enemy, many erected elaborate security systems. The wealthiest of the land built million dollar fortresses with billion dollar maximum security protection. Conversely, even those with little or nothing, invested what they had to possess this intangible commodity called security. Ignorantly playing into the enemy's hand, they constructed elaborate comfort zones for this pernicious antagonist. Thus entangling themselves firmly in his suffocating web.

Fear, therefore, ruled as a self-appointed king. Self-preservation disconnected friends. Suspicion disjointed families. Fortresses supplanted homes. Envy separated neighborhoods. Crime detached cities. Politics estranged states. Missiles and nuclear warheads divided nations. Fear wreaked havoc. Every communication outlet, every advertised product, and every initiative in all arenas had one basic foundation ~ fear.

Deceptive and insidious, fear boldly emerged in every sphere of family, society, culture, finance, health, education, religion, and politics. No longer lurking in the background, he commanded prominence in the highest and lowest places. Working from the inside out, he encroached on unsuspecting and vulnerable hearts. He knew no limits and there was no protection known to man that withstood his treacherous grip.

As king, fear illegitimately seized sovereignty. Beginning as a small seed in the human heart, he eventually exploded in speech and then dictated action. Disguised as a kindly, compassionate grandfather offering comfort, his venomous snare was lethal and contagious. Once he gained entrance, his clasp choked hope, light and life. He darkened the doors of reality with despair, despondency, dejection and depression. And with continuous bombardment, he relentlessly discharged taunting messages to silence all other voices but his.

Yet, in the midst of this environment, there were those who recognized this adversary. Believing in the unseen, they knew that they, "Did not wrestle against flesh and blood, but against principalities, against powers, against the rulers of the darkness in this age, and against spiritual hosts of wickedness in the heavenly places." (Ephesians 6:12) Knowing Adonai Tzva'ot, the Lord of Hosts, the One greater than this hideous, invisible foe, they trusted the WORD of their King. Resolute in their belief, that if this All powerful, All Knowing, All Wise, Sovereign, Omnipresent King of kings was for them, then who dare stand against them. (Romans 8:31) Uncompromisingly surrendered to God, they discovered the maximum security code, resisted this nefarious enemy and watched him scamper away as roaches flee from light. (James 4:7) Deciding to live their lives free from the clutches of this potentially debilitating foe, they did extraordinary exploits that went against the grain of culture. Considered as outcasts in this present world, they stood out and apart. Often appearing weak, foolish, rejected, lonely and insignificant on earth, they were valiant, wise, priceless citizens in the kingdom of heaven.

Knowing this truth, they boldly approached the throne of grace, where they obtained grace and mercy in time of trouble. (Hebrews 4:16) Unmasking this adversary, they saw him as a toothless, precocious kitten, mimicking the roar of a lion. Consequently, the adversary became as a feather, impotently tossed even by the gentlest breeze.

Their unwavering belief in the Word of God, allowed them to see the end from the beginning, and it was always good, victorious and triumphant. (Romans 8:28) Knowing that there was One greater in them than in the world (1 John 4:4), they conquered unchartered territories. They dared to go, in the natural and spiritual realm, where many could never conceive or imagine. Theirs was now a world of maximum security and limitless possibilities. As it was in heaven, so it was now on earth.

The seventy came back jubilant. "Lord," they said, "with Your power, even the demons submit to us?"

Yeshua said to them, *"I saw Satan fall like lightning from heaven.* Remember, I have given you authority; so you can trample down snakes and scorpions indeed, all the enemy's forces; and you will remain completely unharmed. Nevertheless, don't be glad that the spirits submit to you; be glad that your names have been recorded in heaven." (Luke 10:17-20)

CHAPTER 1

# JOURNEY TO L10:18

Pitch black, dense clouds cloaked L10:18. In this realm, only those with eyes conditioned to darkness could see. Hovering between the heavens and the earth, L10:18 was headquarters to twenty-five notorious world influencers. In the thick, dawn of darkness, they met for their tricentennial, one day conference. With each of the twenty-five leading legions of other influencers, and one leading all, their unseen world was a swirl of darkness, deceit and devastation. Always competing, and having their own private agendas, these gatherings were ridiculed and detested by the attendees. Nonetheless, they participated if for no other reason than to spy on each other with the intent to guard their territories, showcase their greatness, and hopefully flex their muscles enough to eventually overthrow the leader.

Able to agree on few topics, this unscrupulous group decided to title themselves the executive council/advisor leaders. Wanting to disguise the fact that their true motive was to steal, kill and destroy, (John 10:10) they presented themselves as good Samaritans, seeking the welfare of their advisees. Knowing their limitations, the title was most reflective of their job description and the image they wanted to portray. Without dominion or authority, and having no substance, they thrived on influence and presence that were felt but not seen. Always on the prowl for vulnerable, unsuspecting advisees, they and their legions became formidable adversaries, principalities, powers, and rulers of darkness in this world. (Ephesians 6:12) Manipulating spiritual wickedness in high places, they were relentless in their pursuit of their ultimate objective, which was the annihilation of the sons of God.

Self-appointed to the position, they presumed to counsel, advise and assist those created in the image of God. They presented themselves as guardians of light, beauty, knowledge and freedom, but this image was a mere façade to hide their unseen world of darkness, grotesque bondage, distorted wisdom, deceit, and guile. They detested themselves, each other and especially those they counseled.

Despising humanity and each other, the one day, tricentennial conference on L10:18 was the perfect time and place. Though short and infrequent, these conferences always ended in sowing greater discord and stimulating destructive competition among the attendees. In so doing, they always exceeded the leader's expectations. Sensing that time, as they knew it, was drawing to a close, it was imperative that this one day conference, which could possibly be their last, was attended by all executive advisors. Total attendance was imperative. Only the threat of demotion from the elite advisory group secured their presence.

Upon receiving the summons from the leader, each executive advisor fumed and grunted in disgust. Aware of the time and season, they were consumed with expanding the present darkness and attending a conference was untimely, disruptive, and just plain stupid. Nevertheless, retaining their illustrious status meant more to them than anything else. It was, therefore, with much contempt that they made the journey to L10:18.

# CHAPTER 2

# THE JOURNEY

Chuckling to himself, Fear Monger said, "I will be crowned king one of these days. Everyone knows that I'm the most dominant and have usurped all authority and presence. I have the world in the palm of my hands and they will feed on whatever I throw them. I don't need anyone trying to tell me what to do. This time I'll show them. I stand alone."

Arrogant Pride, who was travelling on the same path, saw Fear Monger approaching. Rolling his eyes, said, "I can't stand his boasting and false humility. I'll shut him up this time and send him quaking in his boots."

Deliberately making a sharp left turn, he zoomed in front of Fear Monger and stopped inches from him. Fear Monger stood dead in his tracks just before plummeting into Arrogant Pride. His heart beating in fear, he cleared his squeaky voice and said, "Hey, watch where you're going. You almost ran into me."

Despising his weakness and the terror he saw in Fear Monger's eyes, Arrogant Pride inched even closer to assert his self-appointed dominance and grunted, "I see you haven't changed. Still the pitiful, fearful coward that you are." He then let out a hideous laugh as Fear Monger backed up, with his shoulders drooping in terror. "When will you get it, you silly fool, you are what you do. Don't ever try to look smug with me, you spineless coward."

Trying to resist the intimidation, Fear Monger was at a loss for words, but somehow managed to eke out a whimper of reply, "You, you don't scare me. Get out...out of my way."

Being the bully that he was, Arrogant Pride stretched out his formidable, snake like figure. Towering over Fear Monger, he sarcastically snarled, "Did you say something? I can't hear you." Beginning to berate his colleague, he shouted, "You may scare those humans, and only Pod (prince of darkness) knows why. It's certainly not because of you. Just look at you!" he shouted. "You are the greatest mystery of all and a disgrace to our executive rank." Now within touching distance, looking down at Fear Monger, he growled in obvious disgust, "How you, a despicable coward, could instill fear in anyone is beyond my comprehension." Continuing his bullying, he barked, "You're nothing but a weak, fearful, scared bunny. I see you're already shaking in your boots. I don't have time to waste on you. Just remember who you are and who I am. Is that clear?"

Receiving no reply, Arrogant Pride raised his tone and bellowed again in Fear Monger's ear, "Is that clear?"

Summoning as much courage as he could muster, Fear Monger lifted his face while still avoiding eye contact and scampered away without responding. Always an admirer and follower of Pod, (prince of darkness) Fear Monger usually lurked in the shadows seeking opportunities to scare his colleagues. What began as a playful joke, became a habit and shortly rooted as a passion.

Realizing his unassuming talent to instill fear in those he considered inferior to himself, Pod promoted him to the highest position as a leadership advisor on his executive team. His colleagues, however, soon realized that Fear Monger's ability to instill fear was his mask to coverup his own fearful nature. Nonetheless, considering humanity inferior to himself, he achieved extraordinary success and fed off of their response to his fearful tactics. Now efficaciously leading legions of fearmongers, he hoped to finally get the respect from his colleagues he felt he deserved. Despising his reaction to Arrogant Pride's taunting comments, he stiffened his resolve to prove to the team that he was a force to be reckoned with.

# CHAPTER 3

# THE RACE

Often travelling in close proximity to Fear Monger, Agony Tormenson paused long enough to overhear some of Arrogant Pride's criticism. Even though they were close relatives who socialized in the same circles, they despised each other. However, knowing that they shared common DNA (Deoxyribonucleic acid), each pretentiously tolerated the other. Ashamed of Fear Monger's cowardly response, Agony Tormenson resisted the temptation to run over his cousin. Stopping within earshot of Fear Monger, unable to disguise his infuriation, he asked, "When will you get it, Fear? You don't need to be what you do, you sniveling coward. But because we're related, you can count on me to finish what you're so incapable of completing yourself. Why, oh why must you be so pitiful and weak? Come on, let's travel to L10:18 together."

Always feeling as if he walked in his cousin's shadow, Fear Monger summoned up the courage and stated, "I'm fine, Agony. I prefer to finish the journey alone. It's good enough knowing that you're never too far behind to reinforce my messages."

Somewhat taken aback by this statement, Agony Tormenson retorted, "Are you insinuating that I'm always behind you? If I am, it's because you're always bumbling and fumbling your way forward. And you get in my way of doing what I do best. You know you're nothing without me, don't you? Without me you're nothing but a toothless dog, with its tail wagging its head. Arrogant Pride was right. You are a fearful fool."

Knowing that his cousin would antagonize and torment him for the rest of the trip, Fear Monger thought of ways to encourage him to leave him alone. Just as he was about to surrender, as he usually did, to his relentless torment, Deceptive Liar approached. Always within earshot of the two cousins and seeking opportunities to interject her perception in every circumstance, she sweetly remarked, "I see you two are deep in conversation. You know there's a reward waiting for the first ones to arrive. Let's not waste time, Arrogant Pride is way ahead. We must catch up with him. He's always first. Perhaps this time, we will beat him at his own game."

Unknown to Fear and Agony, Deceptive Liar saw Arrogant Pride chatting with his sidekick, Illusive Control. Knowing that she always arrived ahead of Fear and Arrogant Pride, she wanted to trick them into a race she usually always won. Hypnotized by her enchanting voice, effervescent personality and irresistible attractiveness, they gazed at her magnificence. As they stood gazing at her mesmerizing beauty, she took off, laughing and speeding ahead. Leaving a trail of iridescent specks of darkness, her two admirers smiled as they watched her leave their sight and disappeared into thick blackness. Moments later, realizing that they fell into her deceitful web once again, Fear and Agony remarked in delightful disgust, "She did it again." Stumbling over each other, they took off in hot pursuit.

CHAPTER 4

# THE DETOUR

Not wanting to be outwitted, again, by Deceptive Liar and Arrogant Pride, Fear Monger released an anonymous message into the atmosphere. "I just saw flashes of light invading the path ahead. It must be a squadron of heavenly angels, perhaps our enemy, Michael, has set a trap for us. If I were you, I would avoid that path. He's probably been sent to destroy us." Immediately reacting to the message, all but four attendees made a sharp turn to the right and some to the left in an attempt to avoid the light at all costs. Accelerating their speed, they scurried away in different directions into the darkness.

Pausing for breath, Arrogant Pride examined the random, incredulous, anonymous nature of the message. As he pontificated further, he concluded that the message might be a hoax sent to instill fear and trigger panic. The more he dwelled on the thought, the more he was convinced that Fear Monger was the culprit. Shaking his head at his gullibility in accepting the truth of the message without validating it, he stormed ahead in disgust. His pride, however, would not allow him to admit that he allowed

Fear to dictate his decision. Being a bold risk taker, he decided to get back on the most direct path to L10:18. As he did, he saw Deceptive Liar ahead. Catching up to her, he asked, "Did you see any light ahead?"

Laughing hilariously, she answered, "Now, you of all people should know that Fear can't fool me. I'm always one step ahead. I instigated his deceitful manipulation as soon as I heard his message. I'm surprised you're asking the question."

Always puffed up with pride, he arrogantly replied, "Don't be foolish. Of course, I saw through his fearful tactic or I wouldn't still be on this direct path now would I? I'm only asking to confirm my suspicion, not because I'm fearful. Remember who I am?"

Not waiting for a reply, he fled, emitting a stench of putrefied sulfur to repel anyone on his trail. However, still disgusted by his momentary weakness, he vowed to take revenge on Fear Monger as soon as time and opportunity allowed.

Fear, in the meantime, took full advantage of his colleagues' response. He fluttered around giggling to himself and said, "I haven't lost my touch. Even with those who know me best, they still respond to my suggestions. If they only knew." Then laughing heinously, he saw Agony Tormenson approaching from behind. Trying to blend into the deep darkness, Fear hoped he would pass him. Now, no longer concerned about being one of the first to arrive on L10:18, he was more anxious not to be terrorized by Agony.

Agony on the other hand, was even more committed to staying as close to Fear as he could. Seeing Fear in the distance, he made a beeline in his direction. Approaching him slowly, (because

Fear was known to be unpredictable), he said, "I know you're trying to hide from me. You should know better cousin. I'll always be right by your side, if not on your trail. I need you as much as you need me. The way I see it, you plant the seed, and I water it. We're in this together. Now, how about if we finish this journey and pretend that we're friends as well as cousins?"

Steadying his easily shaken nerves, Fear replied, "Only if you promise not to bully me along the way."

"I give you my solemn word, you pretentious coward," Agony answered. "You can trust me as much as I trust you."

Resigning himself to endure whatever torment his cousin had planned, he resumed his journey in fear and trembling, expecting the unexpected, and not knowing what that might be. With their destination now in sight, Fear exhaled in anticipation of relaxing under Pod's protection. However, before they arrived on L10:18, Arrogant Pride, who was always a step ahead, stood waiting at the gate.

CHAPTER 5

# AT THE GATE

Seeing Arrogant Pride's pompous, imposing figure leaning across the entrance to L10:18, Fear turned to Agony and said, "We need to cut him down to size once and for all. Let's exchange places. We look so much alike; he won't recognize the difference. We know his pride and arrogance is nothing but hot air. Even so, I'm no match for him, but you are, cousin."

Always up for a challenge, Agony Tormenson asked, "What do you have in mind?"

"If we can strip away his title, or at least make him believe that he no longer has one, then we can strip away everything else. He'll be rendered powerless," replied Fear.

Rubbing his hands together at the anticipation of deflating Arrogant Pride, Agony said, "Brilliant idea. But we don't need to make an adversary of Arrogant Pride. He's a necessary partner with us."

"Don't remind me," Fear whispered. "But I know exactly who is perfect for this task. He asks no questions and is always available when I call. Just the mention of his name silences all of my adversaries."

"You don't mean 'Death Threat,' do you?" Asked Agony with a malicious grin on his face.

"He's the most terrifying fear of all in our arsenal. Not even Arrogant Pride can stand against him."

"Exactly my point. And because he's not an advisor, he can make a cameo appearance and bring Arrogant Pride down a notch or two," Fear responded with unusual confidence.

"I see your point," responded Agony. "Let's not waste time. Any threat against you is a threat against me. We're in this together."

Looking at Agony suspiciously, Fear held his breath for any sudden agonizing attacks from his cousin. Recalling that the only time they worked together in harmony was when they were attacking or defending themselves from a common foe, Fear relaxed. Then sending a silent signal that only Death Threat heard, Fear and Agony waited, boldly glaring at their adversary. Within moments, Death Threat appeared.

After a brief exchange with Fear and Agony, he quietly slid towards Arrogant Pride. And catching him unawares, he rolled himself in a thick, black, smoldering smoke, even darker than the environment on L10:18 and engulfed Arrogant. Without warning, Arrogant Pride's usually inflated form deflated and began flailing about within the black smoke. Fear and Agony began laughing hysterically as they watched Arrogant desperately attempt to escape Death Threat's clutches without success. In the meantime, other Executive Advisors began arriving at L10:18's entrance. Worthless Shame; Confused Perception; Disgrace Humiliation; Gossip Slander and Callous Religion were among the first to arrive. Each witnessing Arrogant Pride's fall.

# CHAPTER 6

# ARROGANT PRIDE

Collapsed and flattened by Death Threat, Arrogant Pride's humiliated form lay prostrate at the gate. Relishing the opportunity, those attending the conference were eager to step on his deflated form as they entered L10:18. As Callous Religion dug her heels into his deflated form, she muttered, "Finally, he's getting what he deserves. I saw this coming for some time. Perhaps now he won't be so smug."

Likewise, Gossip Slander was bursting with delight and couldn't wait to broadcast what she witnessed. Thinking of how to embellish the story to further his degradation, she took mental images of his humiliation. She then began propagating his shame to other legions with insatiable appetites to steal, kill and destroy, even among themselves.

Notwithstanding his disgraced, embarrassed, dejected and dispirited state, Arrogant Pride was determined to endure this experience with as much ego as he could muster. Resisting the urge to summon his legion of others bearing his arrogant image for assistance, (because his pride would not permit it), he compelled himself to move forward. Stiffening his countenance, his snake like form began shifting. And with his tail tucked around his head, he finally limped beyond the gate and into the conference grounds.

Waiting in the shadows was one of his closest friends and companions, Narcissistic Delusion. Seeing his friend in such disgrace, Narc D. (so called by his friends) reached out and said, "I really wanted to give you a helping hand back there, my friend. But everyone was moving so fast I didn't have a chance." Continuing, he asked rhetorically, "You know you're one of my favorites, right?" In reality, knowing that Arrogant Pride was one of Pod's relatives, Narc D. saw an opportunity to feign concern hoping to further his good standing with Pod.

Suspicious of all his colleagues Arrogant Pride replied, "I don't need your help. I believe you know I have legions at my beck and call. It's not as bad as it looks. In fact, this experience will make me stronger, better and wiser than before. Just wait, time will tell."

Narc D. replied, "I couldn't agree with you more. I can tell the difference already." Then changing the subject, he inquired, "Do you know what this conference is all about? I expect recognition for all the outstanding work that I've done in the last few decades covertly infusing narcissism in every area of humanity. Because of me, the definition of love and freedom have drastically shifted. And we all know that's the basis for everything else."

Infuriated with his self-aggrandizement, Arrogant Pride grunted, "Not if I have any say in it. But who knows, anything is possible." Believing that Pod had reserved a seat at his right

hand, as he often did at previous conferences, Arrogant said, "I prefer you go in ahead of me."

Perceiving this as a compliment, Narc D. was only too pleased to march ahead of Arrogant. As they entered separately, Arrogant with his head stretched as high as it could go, slithered to the head of the table, believing that a seat was preserved for him, only to find it was already occupied by Lawless Destroyer.

# CHAPTER 7

# POD

Like cats in a Halloween parade, the conference was a nest of vipers, each vying for dominion, authority and presence. The open space was chaotic, disruptive and frenzied. The stench of putrefied sulfureted fumes filled the black atmosphere as the attendees emitted puffs of thick, dark, venomous smoke that angrily swirled upward as a rising tornado. The stage was almost set. Being a clever disguiser of many personas, characters and costumes, Pod chose the one he knew commanded immediate subjugation and fear. Therefore, knowing that his faithful dependents could not tolerate light, he adorned himself in his most intimidating and beguiling appearance. Glowing with the darkest of light in deep shades of purple, red, grey and midnight blue, he reflected the darkness as a beacon of reflective blackness.

Purposely delaying his entrance, but ensuring that even in his absence, his presence was felt, he increased sound to its highest levels of discord. Watching his followers squirm and squeal in delight as the noise levels and dissonance amplified, Pod made his grand entrance. The environment morphed into greater darkness as all-consuming, incomprehensible malevolence overpowered every other presence in the space. His diabolical manifestation rendered everyone else silent. Intimidated by his vile aura, they were reminded of why they were enslaved and ensnared in his malicious vice.

Many covered their eyes that were burning from the indescribable acidity of his stench. Others shrank in fright as the putrid smoke of his hot breath engulfed them. Some bold enough to remain upright, stood transfixed, hypnotized by his gruesome stature. The experience was terrifying yet exhilarating. They all aspired to his level of perceived greatness. Awakening as if from a dream, the room began to thunder with loud, agonizing grunts of applause. The louder the grunting, the more animated they became. Mass pandemonium exploded as they began screaming, thrashing, and writhing as if in excruciating, uncontrollable agony. This continued for some time, as Pod devoured the drunkenness of their worship. When the chaos subsided, he yelled out "More...more...more."

As he called for more, the attendees began screeching and attacking each other in frenzied abandonment. The space was filled with thunderous activity, as each attendee attempted to exceed the evil of the other. Still shouting, "More...more...more," Pod laughed at what he considered their childish attempts to gratify his insatiable hunger. Knowing that it was a futile attempt, he propelled his hot, dragon like breath across the atmosphere that rendered the attendees as docile doves fluttering in a tropical breeze. The meeting was ready to begin.

CHAPTER 8

# THE ONE DAY CONFERENCE

Compelling dire submission, Pod allowed a moment of silence before he began. Blinded by his dark, mesmerizing beauty, his leadership team gazed at him in awe and wonder while salivating for an opportunity to overthrow his dominion. Being a devoted slave was not enough. Reflecting his image merely scratched the surface. They wanted to be him. Suspecting their evil thoughts, Pod ruled with a tightly closed fist that allowed them no latitude to think on their own. His was complete domination. In his realm and under his rulership, self-will was not an option. It was either his will or none at all. His followers knew it, and they willingly surrendered.

Ensuring that he made eye contact with everyone, Pod began the meeting. Knowing that he had captivated their attention and silenced all other voices, he began with a ferocious, barely audible groan that was first felt, then heard. Known as the accuser of the brethren, (Revelation 12:10) he viciously grunted in his familiar, accusing tone:

"It's time to stop playing games you sniveling cowards. Time is running out and we haven't even begun to dominate and annihilate humanity as we ought to. Many believe we're a joke, or that we don't exist. And many who dare believe, see us as a childish Halloween pretender dressed to scare babes and fools. Little do they know that we play a deadly game that ends in death. Even worse, many are defecting to our enemy's camp. We can't have that, can we?" He snarled, spewing his burning breath forward as he glared at his audience in unmasked abhorrence. Continuing in the same tone, he shouted, "We must stop the flow of defectors. It's not enough that we destroy a majority at conception. We need more! It's not enough to have even one defect from our clutches. We must retain all we already have and add to our numbers. We need more! In these last days, I command you to lead your legions to seek, and don't stop seeking, until you destroy all infidels who bear any other image but ours."

As the father of lies, (John 8:44) his words flowed effortlessly and convincingly. Continuing his tirade, he barked, "Remember, light can never overcome darkness. So, don't be afraid of light. Look at how darkness has overcome light in this present age. But we need more! We need more! We need more!" He shouted and proceeded, "Since I can't be everywhere, I have commanded Lawless Destroyer and his legions to take the lead under my authority. The enemy is increasing. Therefore, we must increase. Moving forward, all of you, every one of you must take your orders from Lawless Destroyer. If not, as he is so named, he too shall destroy you, strip away your title and whatever authority you think you might have. You know me, this is not a threat, this is a promise. When we leave here, we need to be on the same mission, led by Lawless Destroyer.

Under his leadership, and my guidance, he will instigate dissonance, disunity and destruction in families, friends, neighborhoods, cities, states, and nations. He will destroy every known system, ideology and structure established by man and rewrite history. We take no prisoners. Never forget that we are here to steal, kill and destroy. If there is any other outcome, then we fail and you know what we do to failures. It's them or you."

Pausing to glare at his audience with daggers of hatred shooting from his stare, he asked rhetorically, "Any questions?"

All but one remained still, as hatred, fear and intimidation gushed from Pod's sulfated charisma. Always engrossed in his own arrogance, Arrogant Pride puffed himself up and responded, "I understand perfectly Pod and couldn't agree with you more. However, how do you propose we respond to...I dare not even speak The Name...but we all know what it is."

At Arrogant Pride's mention of The Name, an anguish, guttural cry filled the space and all gasped and hissed in horror. Understanding Arrogant Pride better than anyone, Pod answered, his own arrogance and pride reaching its boiling point, "How dare you even mention the thought of The Name in this meeting. If we weren't closely related, I would crush you to powder and blow you into the wind. Nonetheless, you bring up a valid point. The strategy is the same we've always used, we distract, deceive and then destroy. We distract by leading our despicable charges to question everything, especially the existence and authority of The Name. Then we employ deceit to lead them to our conclusion. And the end is easy. This tactic worked like a charm in that loathsome garden and has never failed. We all know that The Name is just another name unless it is spoken in relationship, dominion, authority and presence with The Person. We know that speaking and believing in The Name alone is not enough." After a hideous, mocking, laugh, he continued, "Even we believe in The Name and tremble. (James 2:19) But that will not deter us from our mission. It's only when we see the relationship, presence, authority and dominion with The Name that we will momentarily back off the attack. Even then, we must choose our fights carefully. If we find the enemy able to resist us, then, and only then, will we flee. (James 4:7) Not a moment sooner. Some of you give up too soon. In this new season, we must relentlessly pursue with all the weapons in our arsenal, by all means possible, with every opportunity we sniff out, until they gladly surrender. Is that clear?"

Not waiting for a reply, he continued, "Lawless Destroyer has already drawn up his battle plans. He has recruited legions of foot soldiers ready to respond to his bidding. Many of them are in high places and occupy seats of power and influence, but we need to add more to strike at our true enemy. Let's not waste time on those already in our camp. We need to hunt the double minded, the lukewarm, the CINOs (Christians in Name Only). We need to go after the very elect themselves. (Matthew 24:24) It might be easier than you think. Let's turn up the heat to its maximum. Our enemy wants us to believe that we will never win this war, but we will destroy as many as we can while trying."

As he ended his oration, the sounds of multiple drums beating in discord sounded in the distance. The noise got louder and more frenzied as it penetrated and shook the darkness as dense, thick black smoke was released. The attendees began reacting to the frequency and started scratching, jumping and contorting their sulfuric vaporous forms with agonizing screeching. As the frequency increased, so did their anarchic response. Pod grunted in demonic delight and began bellowing, "More! More! More!" His cohorts joined in the chant, as they exploded in tumultuous applause.

CHAPTER 9

# DEPARTING L10:18

Invigorated by their rapturous response, and wanting the momentum to last beyond the conference, Pod made one final act. Reproducing his image, he engulfed his devoted slaves in his vaporous frame. He then opened his dragon like mouth and spewed out his fiery breath that swirled like lightning above, below and through them. His voice now as a thunderous waterfall, speaking assertively as the father of lies, he stated, "I know many of you want to be me. Now you are me, and I am you. You are to bare my image on earth and in all humanity. Every life matters. Never, ever give up, until you see my likeness reflected in every arena of life, people and culture. When the final battle is over, we will be the ones left standing. And I, I will be exalted in your midst."

Another outburst of hissing filled the environment. Lingering as he inhaled the adoration, Pod's presence slowly dissipated.

Drunk with anticipation of greatness, each attendee heard what they wanted to hear. And what they heard was that they were the same as Pod (Prince of Darkness). Each felt empowered.

They were unstoppable. Feverish with excitement, they stumbled over each other trying to get back to their own domain and convey the exhilarating news to their legions. The urgency to exit L10:18 created a whirlwind of entanglements. Always competing, the attendees contorted, slithered, and scuttled to be the first to leave and the first to demonstrate their newfound dominion, authority and presence with Lawless Destroyer as their newly appointed general.

Wanting to distinguish himself, Fear Monger messaged the other advisors, "Be careful as you go. It's reported that heaven's archangel, Michael, has set many traps for us. Take a different path to avoid conflict."

Familiar with this fear tactic, Arrogant Pride cynically responded, "Can't you come up with a new fear tactic? Not this time, Fear Monger. I'll go the way I want to." Having said this to keep up appearances, he then decided to take another path, just to be on the safe side.

With each lost in their own world, they sprinted towards their compound of legions who were eagerly awaiting news from the conference. Feeling empowered, unrestrained and free to implement Pod's plan, they ran headfirst into an invisible wall. Attempting to bypass the wall, they quickly discovered that they were individually boxed in and trapped with no means of escape and no means of communication.

# CHAPTER 10

# CORRALED

Momentarily forgetting that there was greater dominion, authority and presence than Pod's, the advisors were stunned to have so quickly fallen prey to their enemy's trap. Unknown to his devotees, Pod was the first to hit the wall, followed by Arrogant Pride and the remainder of the clan, including Lawless Destroyer. Fear Monger and Agony Tormenson were surprisingly the last to crash. Closed in on every side, all they could do was silently wait for Pod to provide a means of escape. Unknown to them, although their conference was held under the cover of darkness, in what they presumed was their secret place, it was vibrantly illuminated in heaven's celestial light.

As the Kingdom of Heaven watched the conference, the King of Heaven's armies, commented:

"Why are the nations in an uproar,
the peoples grumbling in vain?
The earthly kings are taking positions,
leaders conspiring together, against Adonai and His anointed.

They cry, "Let's break their fetters.
Let's throw off their chains!"
He who sits in heaven laughs,
Adonai looks at them in derision.
Then in His anger He rebukes them, terrifies
them in His fury.
...Therefore kings, be wise, be warned, you judges
of the earth.
Serve Adonai with fear; rejoice, but with
trembling."
(Psalm 2:1-5)

Knowing that it was not the time, but that the time was near, the King of Heaven stated, "Answered prayers are in progress."

Instantly responding to his command, Michael dispatched a small squadron of warring angels to L10:18. And in the twinkling of an eye, they erected an invisible wall around the dark realm.

Trapped in solitary confinement, Pod began appealing to God for an audience. Knowing that with God's unconditional mercy and unlimited grace, he would receive the answer to his appeal, he began preparing his accusations. A chameleon by choice and character, he was best known as the accuser of all, including Elohim Himself. Accusing was the bread and butter of his existence. Therefore, he sought every opportunity to justify himself and his evil choices by accusing others. Then on a day, like any other, when the sons of God came to present themselves before the Lord, that Pod was summoned to present himself before Him also. (Job 1:6 & 2:1)

An outcast in the Kingdom of Heaven, he had no means of entrance other than by invitation only. Therefore, in the twinkling of an eye, he was escorted from L10:18 to another realm of unapproached light (1 Timothy 6:16) With closed eyes and bowing low (for he couldn't endure the light), it appeared that he was humbling himself before the King of kings. Unknown to him, his false humility was exposed by the very light he shunned. Cognizant that he was in his enemy's domain, he tread carefully and took a subservient role that he despised. Reminded of Adonai's sovereignty, he waited in silence, until he received the invitation to speak. Then came his turn to stand before the throne of Judgement.

Knowing that he was the father of lies, the Lord asked a rhetorical question, "From where do you come?" (Job 1:7)

True to his self-created lying character, Pod answered nonchalantly, "From going to and fro on the earth, and from walking back and forth on it." (Job 1:7)

The Lord replied, "I know for that's all you and your cohorts can do, is to roam back and forth as a roaring lion seeking whom you may devour." (1 Peter 5:8) Then cutting to the chase, He confronted him and said, "You know I see and know all. Nothing is hidden from my sight. Now is not the time to unleash the Lawless Destroyer. There is an appointed time and season for that, but it is not now."

Forgetting whom he was addressing, Pod asked in an accusatory tone, "Why are you still protecting those humans of yours?" Without waiting for a reply, he continued, "Even you know they crave evil above all else. They are begging for lawlessness. I'm just giving them what they want. Surely, you won't deny me this. I'm actually doing You a favor and allowing them to exercise their free will. After all, You created them with the ability to choose and right now, they are choosing me and my kingdom. I know you're a jealous God, but even You cannot violate your own word."

Always seeing through his rhetoric, the Lord emphatically stated, "Go. I will determine the time and season when you and your leadership team will be released."

CHAPTER 11

# ACCUSATIONS

Making a final point, Pod declared with arrogance, "I know You are merciful and gracious, slow to anger and abounding in unconditional love and faithfulness...And You have not dealt with us according to our sins. Nor punished us according to our iniquities." (Psalm 103:8-10) But even You must admit defeat at some point. They prefer me to You."

He who sits in heaven laughed and looked at him in disdain. (Psalm 2:4) Then He issued a command, "Keep them in confinement until the right time."

As he was being dragged away, Pod could be heard screaming, "You're not fair! You're the liar! How could You go back on Your word and take away humanity's free will? They want me! They don't want or need You. Where is Your mercy? Where is Your compassion? You're a phony. You're the destroyer. Taking away joy, happiness, and everyone's freedom to define love. I know it and they know it...They want me...they want me...All I want to do, is to give them what they want. Just let me give them what they want…" His whimpering trailed off as he was dragged, kicking and screaming, back to L10:18.

The moment his presence broke through the thick blackness of L10:18, he regained his austere, prideful composure. Back in solitary confinement, he released a subliminal message to his cohorts also in confinement, "I've got exciting news to share. Just returned from a meeting with The Name we do not mention. He's still wrapped around my finger and will do whatever I say. While we are detained here for a short while, He won't keep us here long for He knows His time is short. In the meantime, let's make the best use of our time and plan our next attack against Him and His anointed. The good news is that our legions are still unleashed on earth to do our bidding. While we cannot directly command their actions, we can indirectly steer them in the right direction as they implement our plans as they were taught. Our communication with each other and with them may be delayed, but have no fear, we will rise again, stronger and more determined than ever. Earth will be as ripe fruit falling before us, begging for relationship and guidance. We will not fail them. Have faith my loyal subjects. We shall win in the end."

No sooner after the twenty five leaders received the message from Pod, they forwarded an abbreviated version to their respective legions. "Delayed on L10:18. Continue the work with even more vigor. We will be back to ground zero soon."

With their commander-in-chief and generals missing in action, the lower level earthbound troops on ground zero vied for leadership. Mayhem erupted as they competed for who had the greatest impact and therefore who should be in charge. Like rebellious students when their teacher is absent, these junior imps assumed control. Each believing that their respective function was the most essential to their kingdom mission to steal, kill and destroy, their internal battle rose to new heights of ferocity.

As their frenzied internal battle raged, conflict on earth increased. Wars and rumors of wars ran rampant. Nations rose against nation, and kingdom against kingdom. There were famines, pestilences, and earthquakes in various places. Many sons of God were delivered up to tribulation and to be killed. Betrayal was commonplace, and hatred became the mantra of the day. During this time, those being mentored under Deceitful Liar's leadership elevated in rank and became dominant contenders for governance in their kingdom. As a result, many false prophets emerged and deceived many sons of God. And even though Lawless Destroyer was not fully unleashed on the earth, the love of many grew cold, as deceit, hatred and lawlessness abounded. (Matthew 24:6-12) As it was in the kingdom of darkness, so it was on earth. However, still not acknowledging the presence and influence of the unseen kingdom of darkness, many wrestled against flesh and blood. (Ephesians 6:12)

# PART TWO

. . .

# INTRODUCTION

# OWN

Following a seven year period of global chaos, as demons instigated havoc on earth, the earth mysteriously quieted. Earthquakes, floods, fires, erupting volcanoes, tsunamis, wars, mysterious diseases; unexplained deaths; famine in fertile places, and countless other disasters, all labeled as 'acts of god,' ceased as suddenly as they began.

With the silence and sudden inactivity from the unseen world, humanity boldly proclaimed themselves the victor. 'Acts of god,' were declared the predator and the idea of god became the number one opponent. It was now time for healing. Peace and security were the two commodities everyone needed but only few found. Humanity clamored for worldwide unity as the obvious choice to withstand the unseen forces that threatened obliteration. Believing that unity was better than division, national leaders bonded as one, under one banner, with one agenda, i.e. world peace. Consequently, the United Nations emerged as the one world ruling power.

Rebranding themselves as the Global Union (GU), their first order was to erase indelible

lines of geographic and continental divisions.
With an open map, world geography was
renamed East, West, North and South. Former
continents, countries, flags, history, culture and
religions were annihilated. In a world without
borders, it was the GU's mandate and
responsibility that the earth's population was
evenly dispersed. Therefore, under the
administration of the GU, people were relocated
and lived where they were told. Everyone was a
global citizen and all individual, distinguishable,
dividing lines became obsolete, including, racial,
ethnic, cultural, gender, religious and sexual
differences.

Desiring peace above all else, humanity
celebrated their global identity, fortifying
themselves against unseen, external forces they
defined as an enemy of the GU. The idea of god, if
it existed, was labelled their one and only
offender. They, therefore, vigorously wrote it out
of history, rendering it a figment of humanity's
insipid imagination.

Appointing themselves as creators and
independent owners of the visible and invisible
realms, humanity assumed the title of 'gods.' Led
by one person leading a small group of power
hungry, depraved, and cowardly regimes, the
world inconspicuously transitioned into its new
global era.

Having a charismatic, mesmerizing
personality, people clamored for this global
leader's brand of One World with One Voice.
Offering peace, redistribution of the world's
resources, along with mandatory acceptance and
approval of individual choices from a radical yet
meticulously crafted menu, this leader's message

came upon the heels of desperate need and overwhelming fear.

Together as one, just as in the days of Nimrod, they believed that everything they conceived was possible. Their short term visibility, magnified by their scientific, technical, microchipped, artificial intelligence, resulted in a world of smoke and mirrors, copies and counterfeits, and types and shadows of creation. Therefore, owning their destiny, they attempted to achieve the inconceivable and boldly proclaimed earth as heaven, and heaven as earth.

Utopia was on their horizon. Even death was proclaimed an illusion in their neatly ordered world (N.O.W). In this N.O.W. many looked but could not see. They heard but did not listen. They were awake yet unconscious to any other reality but the visible. Therefore, living within walls of state induced imprisonment, humanity touted victory over invisible forces.

Now was a timeless season of one: one earth; one global nation; one ideal; one god (self); one vision; one leader; one army; one family; one voice; one language; and one gender. In this season of 'one', legitimate life was conceived outside the womb with planned parenthood at the helm. Each new life was systematically injected at birth with the GU nanochip, and every life was counted, monitored, and surreptitiously controlled.

The majority of this N.O.W generation was born following a season of chronic anxiety, without knowledge of liberty or historical truth. Like zebras in a parade, they were the nameless, faceless, gender neutral hypnotized generation with voices but no speech. In contrast, the new norm was unbelievable to the older generations who vaguely remembered the former days. Yet, survival required the altered state of reality to which people readily adjusted.

Freedom was redefined as conformity. Truth became relative and everyone craved for their brand of peace and security at any cost. In this globally manufactured paradise, everyone was a ward of the GU; except for the few ruling elite and a vagabond, illegal, illegitimate, untamable, remnant called deplorables, who lived off the global grid; citizens of heaven living on earth.

Not surprisingly, the church was non-existent. Skylines in every city and state around the world shifted. Steeples were declared treasonous to the neatly ordered world (N.O.W) and ceremoniously torn down. Other historical buildings, paintings and other national monuments treasured in times past were despised, censored and/or destroyed. Historical books were inconspicuously missing having been burned and censored some time before. Nothing of the past remained that reflected a different ideology or a different culture. This N.O.W emerged, as an invincible force signaling the beginning of the end, masking types and shadows of prophesies vaguely remembered from ancient times.

In this tightly controlled N.O.W., the chasm between the ruling 'gods,' and the lesser 'gods,' was immeasurable. Anyone caught worshipping any other than the GU leader was declared a global enemy and quickly terminated. Attempting to erase history, it was repeated. Falling into the same delusion of previous generations, the GU calculated without the only eternal reality, "the Way, the Truth and the Life." (John 14:6)

In this season, heaven was silent. Patiently waiting for the mystery of lawlessness to be fulfilled (2 Thessalonians 2:7) before executing final judgement on the earth. Adonai's Ecclesia prepared and longed for their conquering King.

However, believing that victory over all unseen forces were finally won, the GU celebrated their achievements and declared themselves an impermeable force that nothing above, below or on the earth could conquer. Unbeknownst to them, the final battles were about to begin.

In the eternal now, it was always the right time. Heaven was ready. The **G**od of gods, **L**ord of lords, **K**ing of kings, Adonai Tzva'ot, Yeshua, the Messiah, began arising from His throne. The earth trembled at His movement. The Lion of the Tribe of Judah mounted His stallion and prepared to lead His army in the final battle. With all power, dominion and authority in His hands, (Matthew 28:18), and a double edged sword in His mouth, (Revelation 1:16) He could dismantle earth's pitiful army and weapons with one word. Yet, He chose to battle on their terms, in their time and space. Even so, the outcome was certain. The GU was no match for Heaven's army as there was, is and always will be, One **G**od, One **L**ord, One **K**ing, with One Kingdom. As it is in heaven, so it will be on earth; in the realm of NOW, "...for such a time as this." (Esther 4:14)

"Why are the nations in an uproar,
the peoples grumbling in vain?
The earthly kings are taking positions,
leaders conspiring together, against Adonai and
His anointed.

They cry, "Let's break their fetters.
Let's throw off their chains!"
He who sits in heaven laughs,
Adonai looks at them in derision.
Then in His anger He rebukes them, terrifies
them in His fury.
...Therefore kings, be wise, be warned, you judges
of the earth.
Serve Adonai with fear; rejoice, but with
trembling."
(Psalm 2:1-5)

# CHAPTER 12

# LOCUSTS

Like geese flying in formation, the sky glistened with facets of diamond like brilliance, as squadrons of silver breasted locusts patrolled the airways. These locust like drones, filled the atmosphere. Designed to absorb and redirect external elements from above and within the clouds, they were armed with protective shields ensuring their dominance against sun, rain, hail, snow, wind, thunder, lightning or anything that might threaten the earth below. With built in artificial intelligence, (AI) they had the ability to quickly detect and dismantle foreign objects by magnetically connecting as one glistening shield to form an impenetrable offense and defense.

These locust like creatures were metallic, triangular shaped, each with a distinguishable design that signaled its function within their nest. With retractable wings, they glided effortlessly in their rested state. However, in their offensive/defensive mode, large, spider like wings protracted and had the ability to exchange encoded messages as well as excrete toxic gases as directed. What appeared to be eyes covering their bodies that rotated 360 degrees per second, they scanned the cosmos for signs of foreign invaders. Their ability to launch upward and attack perceivable threats were instantaneous. Likewise, their ability to plunge downward, in any direction, in any weather, at any time, enabled them to serve and protect the earth from attacks above.

Initially designed as harmless programmable carriers, they were first perceived as innocuous drones. In prior evolutionary generations, during a season of global wars and rumors of wars, they were used as carriers of programable germ and nuclear warfare, undetectable, untraceable and self-destructible. Now, in a season of peace, they were upgraded by an ingenious scientist to guard the earth from perceived destructive, natural elements. This included safeguarding that an even distribution of water and light flowed throughout the land. With a programmed built in dimmer switch, they filtered the sun's rays ensuring exact levels of light in precise timing and locations. Therefore, they illuminated or darkened the earth as needed. Gaining dominance and control of where, when and how rain, snow, light and dark affected the earth, humanity believed they had eliminated all vulnerability to 'acts of god,' from above. Consequently, they boldly declared themselves victors over these unseen, and formerly uncontrollable forces.

# CHAPTER 13

# SNAKES

As the silver locusts guarded the skies, titanium snakes defended the ground. These snake like objects had the artificial intelligence, (AI) to plunge deeply into the earth's crust, constantly monitoring movement from beneath. They too had eyes around their spear-like head, and laser-like spikes around their long, tubular bodies. With protractible tails that rotated independent of the head, they had the ability to slither in multiple directions simultaneously.

Burrowing beneath the earth's surface, they detected earthquake epicenters and strengthened gaps of vulnerability to eliminate threats of earthquakes and volcanic eruptions. Built to withstand any temperature, these reptilian like creatures patrolled the ground beneath the surface. Armed with sensors to attack any foreign object that might threaten earth's surface, they were intimidating ground troops.

If threatened, these undetected, slithery titanium snake-like creatures would congregate. Like links in a chain, they would interconnect, forming an inscrutable plate-like shield that fortified the earth's core. Constantly moving through the ground beneath, they also shifted the earth's soil releasing chemicals to enrich the land to produce abundant food, thus eliminating any threat of famine. Farmers, therefore, no longer needed to till the surface from above.

With the silver locusts regulating the water supply from above, and the titanium snakes moving the earth beneath, the land yielded whatever humanity wanted. And like the silver locusts, they were armed with toxic, lethal gases they could release with the push of a button. Finally, humankind gained absolute dominion they sought, and glorified their wisdom and intelligence above all else.

# CHAPTER 14

# FISH

Along with the locusts-like creatures above and snake-like creatures below, a new breed of fish appeared in the oceans. In various shapes and sizes, these steel-like fish were carefully designed to defend the seas from all threats that invaded the land. Constantly on patrol, they had the ability to regulate the current of the oceans, sizes of the waves and managed the oceans' water and salt levels.

So similar were they to the real thing, they were undetectable by the naked eye. Designed in various sizes and shapes mimicking the original creation, these fish-like creatures were indestructible. With protractible tails and eyes that constantly shifted in all directions, they were a terrifying weapon. Relying on their built in sensors and containing lethal explosive gases, they could instantly dismantle any threat, seen or unseen. Programmed with the ability to detect foreign invasion, tsunamis, or any threat to the earth, these creatures, with rocket like precision, could navigate from the ocean's floor, to land or air. They were indeed humankind's masterpiece that guarded the universe from all threat of danger at the touch of a button.

Encoded with an automatic messaging system, these daunting guardians in the air, beneath the earth's surface, and in the oceans, guaranteed security and peace. Theirs was now a neatly ordered world (N.O.W.) and the Global Union (GU) welcomed their seemingly innocuous, benevolent presence. Human defenders were no longer needed as there was only one control center, and one remote controlled master key. And the mastermind of these new creations, and his self-appointed coronation, was quickly approaching.

# CHAPTER 15

# CORONATION

After two years of preparation, the coronation day of the man referred to as 'the savior of the world,' finally arrived. The previous three years on earth were marked with an abundance of food, fun, celebration, and everything appealing to the senses, most importantly peace. During this time, one man emerged as the god-like provider of the abundant life the masses cravenly devoured. His legacy was unmatched. His inventions, ideologies, generosity, charisma, universal identity and familiarity represented every nation, race, gender, color, tribe, language, and sexual choice. He was the complete package in this neatly ordered world (N.O.W.).

In this N.O.W., the timing of the coronation day was strategically planned. After years of turmoil, and the past three years of abundance, security and peace, he sensed a growing restlessness in himself and the masses. So, again with precise timing, he initiated the biggest universal event known in history; his coronation day. Ensuring the masses were fully engaged, he involved them in the planning process, igniting their anticipation of this massive event. This was their first unifying experience since the establishment of the Global Union and he wanted to guarantee that it was spectacular.

In this N.O.W., the globe had become a land without borders, names, flags and identity. As it was in the time of Nimrod, only one technology, communication platform was allowed. And the GU leader controlled it.

The GU functioned as one entity with four equal regions, east, west, north and south. Within the four quadrants, each was responsible for executing the same coronation plan. At precisely the same time, in each time zone, all GU citizens would do the identical thing, i.e., participate in the coronation. The actual and virtual coronation sites were specified.

Wanting to personalize the event, each household received the following invitation from the GU leader:

*Please join me in sharing this special occasion as we coronate each other on our victory over our adversaries. Together, we shall create our own heaven, a world that has never existed, one that surpasses anything that ever was or will be.*

*We will celebrate our achievements, and more to come. We declare that even the sky is no limit and time is irrelevant. Nothing, absolutely nothing, is impossible for us if we only believe. June is the designated month of celebration with the coronation scheduled on the 6th day. So, let us celebrate with carefree abandonment the most important event in the history of the world.*

*Your GU Leader,*
*Magor G. Romind*

With the event only one week away, the earth surged with electric excitement. A global celebration of extraordinary proportion was taking place and there was no limit to the revelry, joy, and fiesta felt by all. Everything flowed in abundance prior to the event, including liquor, food, music, and any activity the masses desired to appease their glutenous and ravenous flesh. It was to be the celebration of celebrations, one that would have an unexpected ending that shocked and provoked uncontrollable laughter in the Kingdom of Heaven.

CHAPTER 16

# RESTLESSNESS

Born during a tumultuous time of global uncertainty, Magor G. Romind, now thirty years old, seized the opportunity to fulfill his forefather's dream of world dominion and authority. Understanding his story from self-proclaimed divine, royal stock, he touted his grandfather's achievements, and unapologetically boasted in his father's accomplishments.

His grandfather, a man of many names, titles and personas, was a notorious terrorist listed on Interpol's top ten most wanted files. First appearing on the horizon as Alexzander T. Kerber, an accomplished scientist, entrepreneur and philanthropist, he gained notoriety as a mass murderer and human trafficker. He experimented with life within the womb to fulfill his dream of propelling humankind to the next evolutionary stage. Following failed attempts, and escaping the law, he changed his identity to Dr. Zenade Aboye and continued with his AI, (Artificial Intelligence), experiments on unsuspecting people. With a high price on his head, and sensing his adversaries closing in, he feigned his own death and escaped justice once again.

Making his next appearance at the Summit of the world elite conference in Panama, he assumed the name of Narzdexael T. Reberk (abb. Narz). Again, narrowly escaping justice, he re-emerged as a mysterious, nameless priest. Having to assume another identity, he resurfaced as a wealthy entrepreneur, founder and leader of the Center Of Self-Enlightenment (C.O.S.E), as Dr. William T. Surrogate. Upon his sudden and crushing death, his estranged son, A. T. Romind emerged. (Ref. Beyond Limits, R7:17: Trilogy - Dominion, Authority, Presence)

Assuming the leadership role of the C.O.S.E., his son, A. T. Romind surfaced as a leader of leaders. With his extreme wealth, domination over global communications and other industries, he was poised to rule the world. Unbeknownst to him, he almost fulfilled his father's diabolical dream of world dominance. However, his untimely and mysterious death, declared as 'an act of god,' intervened. With this history written into his DNA, (Deoxyribonucleic acid), now his son, Magor G. Romind, was determined to finally fulfill his forefathers destiny.

Conceived in a test tube, he did not know his biological mother, had no siblings, no family and no other history or identity but his father's. Having inherited his father's vast empire and all other assets, he became the wealthiest and most influential man in known history at twenty years of age. Despite his youth, he was extremely mature for his age and had one vision. Propelled by his vehement loathing of 'god and acts of god,' he was determined to obliterate it from existence, if it indeed existed, and end its ability to perform any more 'acts' on the earth.

Inheriting his grandfather's scientific mind, he became a master AI developer and created the blueprint for the artificial Locust, Snake and Fish. When the designs became a reality, his dominion was sealed. He not only controlled global communication, but also the world's offensive and defensive systems. His fingerprint was on the remote control and he wielded a power over humankind unlike anyone before him.

With his unassuming charismatic personality, he also led the C.O.S.E., which now had a worldwide presence as the only place of self-worship. Built by his grandfather, Dr. William T. Surrogate, "it was launched as a place of affirmation and encouragement." (Ref. R7:17, Beyond Limits – Presence, Copyright 2020) Having improved the structure, it beckoned even greater attention and admiration than in his grandfather's day.

"The walls were made of hand painted stained glass, with exquisite marble pillars and walkways. It was a modern Sistine Chapel, with massive murals depicting man's evolution on the high, arched ceilings and walls. The carpet was a soft plush burgundy upon which rested ten thousand hand carved, one-of-a-kind, individual burgundy and gold swivel chairs. Enormous exotic paintings framed by burgundy and gold frames honoring the founding fathers of humanism hung on the walls; but the most amazing feature of all was the main aisle.

The center aisle was made of an extremely rare and imported marble, with burgundy and gold rose shaped crystal specks interwoven throughout. The magnificent aisle led to the main platform which was visible from anywhere in the main sanctuary. It was octagonal shaped, made of clear crystal glass that reflected whatever was above it. There were built in lights within the floor and sides of the octagon, and crystal glass covering each side that sparkled in splendiferous display. The platform was electronically wired to ascend and descend with the touch of a remote control that gave the platform an ethereal feel." (Ref. R7:17, Beyond Limits – Presence, Copyright 2020)

Magor G. Romind was the epitome of leadership. Presumably with uncontested dominion, authority and presence, he answered to no one, visible or invisible. Nevertheless, he was not content. There had to be more to conquer, including death and beyond. In the meantime, he craved a larger platform, greater honor and unquestionable worship. The world was not enough. After all, if it were not for his genius, the globe would still be at the mercy of unseen forces they labelled as 'acts of god.'

In this trance-like season of peace and his restlessness growing, he also sensed the same in his subjects. He, therefore, declared his self-appointed promotion to deity and self-proclaimed coronation.

# CHAPTER 17

# BOREDOM

After two years in preparation, with subliminal messages dulling the senses and controlling the mind, people clamored for his coronation. The day finally arrived. Surrounded by his cabinet of twenty-four, everything was ready. Choosing papal-like attire with gold embroidered symbols reflecting the sun, moon and stars, along with every geometric shape, he felt appropriately dressed for the occasion. Having designed his own crown that reflected the headpiece of a king and bishop, inlaid with all manner of precious jewels, he was ready to begin the procession.

The C.O.S.E. was ostentatiously spectacular and the perfect location for his coronation. Replicating the original design, Magor Romind had constructed several C.O.S.E throughout each region. Choosing the West region to host the live event, all C.O.S.E. locations throughout each geographic region held a virtual, live ceremony which every GU citizen was required to attend. Knowing that space was limited within the C.O.S.E., outdoor theatres were also erected to ensure that everyone had a virtual front row seat to this first global, unifying event.

The time arrived. Dressed like a peacock on parade, Magor G. Romind looked impressively at himself. Admiring what he considered an ethereal, god-like, royal, priestly appearance, he smiled at his self-created image of omnipotence and virtual omniscience. Taking a golden scepter in hand, and an ancient looking scroll, he marched ahead of his entourage who were also pompously dressed for the occasion.

The earth hushed in his regal presence. His metallic carriage shimmered as it made its procession to the C.O.S.E. Streets lined with his adoring subjects bowed to him overwhelmed by the majesty of the occasion. Breaking the silence at certain intervals, the people broke into intense applause and chanted in a frenzied stupor, "Our god, lord and king; our god, lord and king; our god, lord and king...." They would then bow as the chanting continued. Then a loud voice broke through and began repeating, "Our g.l.k. Our g.l.k. Our g.l.k."

Hearing the people reciting the initials g.l.k., Magor smiled inwardly and thought, *That's it. That's the title I will adopt. Being king is not enough. I will be the first g.l.k. in history.*

Inhaling deeply, he cherished the moment and wished his forefathers were alive to see this day. Bowing to his subjects as his carriage slowly drove by, his heart swelled with immeasurable pride and power. When he reached the C.O.S.E, people automatically made a pathway and bowed lower as he ceremoniously proceeded into the building.

The Center was filled to capacity. Everyone whom Magor felt worthy to personally witness his coronation was present. He marched forward with his twenty-four cabinet members in tow. Stepping onto the extravagantly adorned platform with all manner of flowers, gold, silver and jeweled ornaments, he slowly approached the podium.

The audience stood in stillness, breathlessly waiting for his first words. Then deliberately taking the ancient looking scroll in his hands, he unfolded it and read:

"In the beginning..." he paused for effect and then continued, "and today is the beginning of beginnings. Whatever was before no longer exists. What exists is what is here today. Our world, all the galaxies, and we, are the only self-chosen, self-existed ones with all dominion and authority. Nothing seen nor unseen shall conquer us. We are the masters of the universe. And I am your leader. Today marks this momentous occasion that will change the course of history."

Then picking up his crown that had been laid before him, he remarked, "With this crown, I am and always will be your beloved one and only god, lord and king, your g.l.k. I will protect you. I will save you. I will provide for you. If you will be my loyal people, I shall give you peace and security. I will provide all your needs." With his tone increasing a crescendo, he ended, "Yes, I am your g.l.k." And placing his self-designed crown on his head, he said with finality and authority, "Now bow and worship me."

In robotic response, the majority of people all over the globe hearing his mesmerizing, authoritative voice, whether in person or virtually, automatically prostrated themselves in worship. Stillness permeated the universe. Waiting for effect, Magor G. Romind broke the silence and shouted, "Now let's celebrate our victory!"

Celebration like never before commenced as all hell exploded in applause. Every form of debauchery, depravity and licentiousness filled the earth as humankind held nothing back from the imagination of their darkened hearts. The drunk and disorderly celebration continued for two months, only ending as the people wearied themselves and they began awaking from their three year stupor. As they did, there was only one question on their hearts, "Now what?"

Magor reveled in a moment immediately following the event. Minutes later, upon removing the robes and crown, he stared at his puny nakedness and was reminded that he was just an average being as any of his species. His discontent returned. And in boredom, asked the same question, "Now what?"

## CHAPTER 18

# NOW WHAT?

With the stench of revelry still in the air, Magor assembled his cabinet and asked the question that haunted him following his coronation, "Now what?"

His right hand cabinet member and closest friend, Zukorain Sedski responded, "It was reported that segments of the GU citizens in all four regions did not attend the event. We're still waiting for the digital report captured by the locust radar identifying who were missing. There's no excuse. Other than death or unconsciousness, everyone had access to virtually attend."

"Do we even care why they did not attend? If they were breathing, they should have been there. Idiots, they forgot that everyone is trackable, anytime and anywhere," another cabinet member added.

"This is treasonous," responded Magor in feigned, offended arrogance. "However, it does present another unifying opportunity. As soon as we know who and where, let's bring charges against them and publicly put them on trial for crimes against the GU."

He then rhetorically questioned, "How dare they, whoever they are, not participate in this event, and not bow down to me? We will make them pay while demonstrating to the GU the consequences of not participating in mandatory events. When will you have the report?"

"I expect them any time now my g.l.k.. What punishment did you have in mind?" Zukorain asked.

"I'm not concerning myself with trivial matters, you decide. I must maintain a neutral, compassionate, and empathetic position," replied Magor. Then continuing said, "Whatever it is, it must be public and the people must be appalled by their treason. Just make sure our global communication reflects my commitment to justice."

"Does this answer your 'what's next' question, my g.l.k.," Zukorain asked.

"It does, but it's still not enough. There must be more," Magor answered.

The twenty-four cabinet members bowed. Another cabinet member, raising his head looked at the g.l.k. for permission to speak, then asked, "Have you thought of a wedding, your wedding? If you want another unifying, celebratory event following the first trial for treason, what's better than a royal wedding?"

The other cabinet members lapsed in silence as they waited anxiously for Magor to respond. Taking time to ponder the proposal, he replied, "Tell me more? Remember weddings and marriages are illegal. I should know. I declared freedom from marriages some time ago. Why would I want to enter into such an antiquated, ridiculous relationship?"

"Remember my g.l.k., you are above the law in all things. Your marriage will be to further unify the GU. Consider if you take a bride from each of the regions to represent your union and commitment to the GU. It would be as if every GU citizen would become your bride and you their faithful husband, my g.l.k. Yours will be the only marriage in the GU, and the preparation for this event will occupy the masses, as did the coronation," replied Ezari Nuka, his third in command, who sat to his left.

"I get the picture. What a dynamic strategy. This will certainly set you apart from all others. Which I believe is what you want. It will surely solidify your g.l.k. status. Not that you need anything, my g.l.k." Zukorain stated with feigned humility.

Silence again filled the room as Magor pondered the suggestion, "Let me consider it." Then sharing his thoughts out loud, he continued, "If the brides were in name only it's feasible, as I don't want to be bothered with relationships. But it's a decision for another day. Now, where's that report listing the names and locations of those who did not attend my coronation?"

Just as he asked the question, a report appeared on each of their monitors. The list was longer than imagined, with almost an equal spread across the four GU regions.

Magor quickly reviewed the list and with finality pronounced, "I want everyone on that list expunged, regardless of reason. Let's make an example of them. I may consider pardoning some as a compassionate gesture but will decide that later. We've got work to do. Report back as soon as you expose and corral these deplorable offenders. They will bow."

# CHAPTER 19

# JOY

Emerging in the shadows of the GU's neatly ordered world, (N.O.W.), were groups of individuals who called themselves the Remnant. Scattered throughout the four quadrants of the GU, they arose from the rubble of the tumultuous season when violence and global chaos prevailed and the idea of a God outside of self, became legally unlawful. Having grandparents and great grandparents who lived during the time when a book called the Bible was universally treasured above all other books, the Remnant recalled the history of the world, and the words, "In the beginning God made the heavens and the earth..." (Genesis 1:1)

Holding onto snippets of ancient stories of faith, they believed in the creator God and the name of Yeshua above all other names. They dared to believe their forefathers account of Yeshua's miracles and His promise to come again to conquer the world and establish His government on earth as it is in heaven. (Matthew 6:10) Nonetheless, without the written word of the Bible, their hearts soared with the knowledge of the unseen God. Having not seen Him, they believed. (John 20:29) Their hearts and all creation bearing witness to His existence.

Knowing the severe penalty for their belief and the deeply rooted hatred of God by the GU, the Remnant, who lived and moved and had their being in Him, (Acts 17:28) lived in the shadows. Because their forefathers did not adhere to the laws of the GU, many of the Remnant were born outside the established system. They, therefore, did not receive the GU's trackable nanochip that was inserted while still in the womb. Yet, there were numerous others of the Remnant, who were born into the GU and had the nanochip inserted into their bodies, whether while in the womb or outside the womb. Notwithstanding, their hearts belonged to the living God. They were counted as citizens of the Kingdom of Heaven and their names were recorded in the Book of Life.

Being led by the Holy Spirit, they moved undetected by the GU. That is, until the coronation day of the self-anointed, g.l.k., Magor Romind. Deciding to bow down to no other God than the One true God, the Creator of Heaven and Earth, many were exposed. Those with the nanochip knew that they would be persecuted for their disobedience to bow and worship the self-crowned g.l.k. They, therefore, prepared themselves to face the consequences. Desiring two things, to hide the word of God in their hearts, and be a witness to their God and Savior unto death, they looked forward to the joy that was set before them. (Hebrews 12:2)

CHAPTER 20

# TREASURE

"I was wondering when the GU would claim our land. We have been blessed that they have left us alone to continue our flower farm." Steffen Marble said to his wife, Charity.

"I wonder what their plans are for the property. I know they have claimed other properties in the area and somehow suspected that ours would be next," Steffen remarked.

"Well sweetheart, we knew this would happen one day. Let's prepare to relocate to their housing community. There's no point in resisting them and even if we did, who is to say that we're also resisting God's purpose for us as well. Remember, He is the Sovereign of our lives and from experience we know that He causes all things to work together for good to those who love Him and are called according to His purposes, (Romans 8:28). This is no exception. Remember, we belong to the Kingdom of Heaven. Everything else here on earth, while they might be important, is temporary, until our true God, Lord and King establishes His kingdom here on earth. (Matthew 6:9-13) So, let's not sweat the small stuff."

"Thanks for that reminder my love. Whatever the consequences, we're in this together. So where do we begin as this house has been in our family since I can remember," Charity replied.

Sighing heavily, Steffen stated, "I've avoided this for the longest, but let's start with clearing out the attic, from top to bottom. I'm afraid to find what's there."

"Let's make it a treasure hunt adventure for the kids. It will be done in no time and we will have fun while doing it," Charity remarked.

"Excellent idea, perhaps others of the Remnant might want to join us as well," Steffen added.

"Let's wait on that, until we're sure we're not putting anyone at risk just by sheer association. We know we're constantly being monitored and we're trackable by the unseen eyes of the GU. I prefer to play it safe," Charity responded.

"I didn't think of that, you're absolutely right. Well then, let's get started," Steffen responded in a familiar matter of fact tone.

Calling their fourteen year old son and ten year old daughter, they then broke the news of their required relocation from their ancestral home. Having been born into the GU system, the children didn't question the change. Their son, Callem asked, "What's the next step, dad?"

"We need to clear out the attic and keep what we want. No need to have the GU burn our valuables, which is usually what they do when they begin clearing out property. No telling what's up there, all we know it's decades of family history and stuff that we need to discard."

"How much time have they given us to move Dad?" his son again asked.

"We received three months' notice, but that doesn't mean much, as they could descend on us at any time. We just need to be prepared," his father responded.

"Well, let's get to it then," their daughter, Kyly added, "This sounds like fun actually. I've always wanted to play up there but you never let me."

Within the next hour, the family opened the hatch door to the attic, climbed the drop down ladder and entered. Adorned with masks and gloves, they delved into the boxes, the drawers, and other miscellaneous discarded stuff and piled them up for the garbage heap. Most were broken and considered useless. Other things such as toys, old computers, phones, moth eaten clothes, household items, and other miscellaneous things were tagged for the trash. Noticing the absence of any literature, the son asked, "I heard of a thing called books that were on paper. I was hoping to find one. I've seen pictures of what they looked like but have never actually seen one."

"Well son," his father replied, you know that before the GU came into power, all literature was destroyed and the penalty was severe if any was found during random searches. I'm sure my father and grandfather burned them all. That's why there aren't any traces of written materials now."

Just as he said that, his wife called out from the opposite side of the attic, "It feels like there's a loose floor board here, honey, can you check it out. I was about to step on it when I felt the boards move under my feet."

"Whatever you do, don't step on it," her husband replied. "The board may have rotted out. Remember when we had the leak in the roof around that area a few years ago, it wouldn't surprise me if the water rotted out the wood. I'll come and take a look."

"Strange, it doesn't look as if the board is rotten, just loose," she replied. Then bending to touch it, and finding that it moved under her hand, she jiggled it again and was able to remove the board. When she did, she gasped in surprise and said, "You won't believe what I just found."

Giving her a signal of silence, her husband whispered, "Let's see what we have here." Having removed surrounding floorboards with the same ease, they uncovered a hidden spot, and to their amazement, there were numerous dust covered books, all with the same title, The Holy Bible.

# CHAPTER 21

# MANNA

Gasping as if discovering gold, the family gingerly lifted the Bibles from their hiding place. To their amazement, the books were in pristine condition. Charity fell to her knees, and looking up whispered, "Thank You, thank You, our amazing God, who provides exactly what we need, when we need it. We've had these books hidden in our attic, now we can know the written word and hide it in our hearts. I've heard of them, now I'm actually holding one in my hands. I can't wait to share it with the others. This is what we've been praying for."

Her husband kissed one of the Bibles and whispered, "This is more important to us than our daily bread. This is Your timeless bread from heaven. Just as You have preserved and protected these books for 'such a time as this,' (Esther 4:14), I know You will do the same for us, no matter what we face. Thank You."

Sensing the importance of the moment, their daughter asked quietly, "So what are we going to do with them?"

"Good question," her father responded barely above a whisper, "For starters, let's get them from the attic and into our moving boxes. I doubt the GU will search through our boxes."

"I know what we can do," Kyly quietly chimed in, "We can disguise them as ornaments and cover them with all sorts of things. I want mine covered with all the dry flowers I've collected from the farm and..."

She was interrupted by an unfamiliar voice shouting from below, "Is anyone home? Is anyone home?"

The family froze in silence hoping whoever it was would go away. However, the barking voice became closer, louder, and more persistent. Steffen motioned to his family and whispered, "Put the books back in the secret place. I'll be right back."

Moving to the entrance of the attic, he shouted, "I'll be right there," and began climbing down the attic stairs.

When he reached the bottom, he saw three men in GU blue and black uniforms pacing the ground floor and taking photos as they went. Steffen said, "I was upstairs. Sorry. I didn't hear you. I didn't even hear your knock."

One of the GU Inspectors sternly replied, "We didn't knock. We don't have to. This is GU property and we can enter at any time. However, we wanted to give you a courtesy shout to let you know that we were here."

"How can I help you?" Steffen asked.

"No help needed. We're here to examine the interior space and assess the contents for your relocation," answered one of the Officers. "We've changed the date and it will be sooner than we thought, perhaps in a week or so."

Inhaling deeply, Steffen responded, "Thanks for the heads up. We're in the process of clearing out the place ourselves."

"No need to do that," another of the GU Inspectors replied. "We will determine what you can keep and what we will repurpose. Your temporary house is almost ready. According to our notes, you and your family will be relocated to temporary housing until we tear this down and rebuild smaller units on the property. When we're finished, you and your family will be relocated back and be responsible for farming a much smaller portion of the land. How many are in your dwelling?"

"There are four of us altogether, but I'm sure you already knew that," Steffen replied.

"Where are they? The house appeared to be empty when we arrived," another GU Inspector asked.

"We were upstairs in the attic, just seeing what's up there," answered Steffen.

"I see," one GU Inspector replied curiously. "And what did you find? You know all property belongs to the GU, so anything you find must be reported. We will take pictures today as we walk through to determine what you can keep. It's better if you and the others are not in the house during this process."

Trying not to arouse suspicion, Steffen replied, "Yes sir, I completely understand."

The men followed him as he reached the entrance to the attic and called his family. As they descended, Charity coughed and said, "It's extremely dusty up there."

The family exited the house as the Inspectors did their assessment. Praying fervently

in their heart for the newly discovered treasures
not to be exposed, they sat in silence and waited.

CHAPTER 22

# GIFTS

Knowing that the GU Inspections were more than an assessment, Steffen shared, "I'm quite sure something triggered our sudden relocation and inspection. Once we're on the GU's radar, they will stop at nothing to prove their point, whatever that may be. Say nothing. Let me do all the talking. Is that clear? And no matter the outcome of this inspection, know that God is with us. Oh, and from now on, we need to be extremely cautious of what we say in the house. Remember, there are meniscal, undetectable eyes and ears in unusual places."

Just as he finished speaking, the Inspectors exited the house and walked towards the family. Holding a stack of unfamiliar papers in his hands, one Inspector asked accusingly, "We found these handwritten copies of a book that mentions another god. Why was it in your house? Where did it come from? Don't you know the penalty for harboring seditious materials?"

Knowing they had planted the papers which was the intent of the inspection and relieved that they did not find the hidden stack of Bibles, Steffen replied, "I don't know how they came to be in the house, but if you say you found them there, then who am I to contradict your statement? Whatever the consequences, I take full and total responsibility, my family is not involved."

As if on cue, another Inspector stated, "I arrest you in the name of the GU. Anything you say will be held against you." Binding his hands and feet in shackles, they then roughly pushed him into their vehicle.

His wife and children stood silently as they watched them take him away. However, before they did, Steffen turned his head and shouted, "It's okay, remember what I just shared. No matter what, I'll see you soon."

Unknown to them, GU Inspectors were following the same procedures throughout each region. Thousands of head of households were arrested simultaneously with the same charge of sedition against the g.l.k. and the GU. Each household randomly selected from a long list compiled by the eyes and ears of the GU of those who did not attend the g.l.k. coronation.

On that day, Steffen, and thousand others from each GU region were transported to a large, enclosed area with numerous cages. Like sheep to the slaughter, they were corralled in these cages, awaiting trial and execution. Preferring to fast and pray, they refused meager portions of bread and water. As they looked up in prayer, silence and stillness prevailed. Nonetheless, indescribable peace rested upon them. Without saying a word, they acknowledged each other as those worthy of experiencing the suffering as their Lord did and looked forward to the joy that was set before them. (Hebrews 12:2) Knowing that theirs was not an ending but a beginning, they prayed more fervently each day for their families and the spreading of the knowledge of the one true God, Yeshua, Jesus Christ, their Messiah. As they silently prayed, those with eyes to see and ears to hear, saw red smoke spiraling upward and knew there was something supernatural among them. Many guards felt a difference they could not explain and showed kindness to their captives. Others, in hatred and anger, wielded their authority and taunted them, saying, "Where is your god now? Whoever he is, he's asleep and has been asleep for some time. There is only one god we acknowledge and we know who he is, and where he is, our g.l.k."

Notwithstanding, whatever the action, it was evident that they were committed unto death to their deeply held beliefs. Heaven applauded and began preparing for one of the biggest revivals in the midst of persecution in recorded history.

## CHAPTER 23

# LIVING EPISTLES

Standing in stunned silence long after the Inspectors took their father away, Charity whispered to her children, "Don't be afraid. God is with him and with us. You know that, so let's remember what he said and be cautious of what we say. I'm sure they planted eyes and ears throughout the house. If you need to speak about anything important, we will do it outside, and even so, we have to speak very quietly, as there are eyes and ears above and beneath us that may be recording what we say and do. Remember the key words we taught you in sign language? Let's begin using it, and even that we need to somehow disguise. Thank Abba that they didn't find the true treasure. We've got work to do."

Still shocked in silence, the children nodded. With tears streaming down their faces and holding tightly to their mother they returned to the house. Over the next four days, they silently removed the Bibles, sewing them into their clothing, placing them in unusual containers such as cakes, pans, and flowerpots with small plants as covering, and gift wrapping others.

Knowing their movements were trackable, the Remnant met randomly under the guise of various celebratory occasions, such as birthday parties and anniversaries, which were permitted by the GU. The only stipulation was that no more than fifteen citizens were allowed to congregate at any given time.

At the appointed time and location of their weekly 'celebratory' event, the Marble family gathered their gifts in disguise and headed out. Presuming that they were being watched, they moved cautiously. With flowerpots in hand, a cake and covered pots and pans, they began their journey. Arriving at their destination, they were welcomed by their hosts. With news of numerous individuals in their region arrested for sedition blasting on all communication outlets, along with names and locations, everyone at the gathering were especially guarded. Very little was exchanged until they entered an empty basement designed to muffle sound. A set of drums was the only item in the room, and with music in the background, they began their meeting.

After exchanging hugs and tears, as several members of the group were arrested, along with Steffen, they began worshipping and praising God. They prayed fervently for their loved ones and for the Word of God to spread even more rapidly despite the present persecution.

When they were done praying, Charity shared their finding in the attic and began handing out the gifts wrapped in unusual containers. Many gasped in awe as they held a Bible for the first time. Having heard of it, and knowing many stories passed on through the ages, they were now finally holding the Word in their hands. For many, it was as if the Word had become flesh and they were holding on to the ultimate author of the book, Yeshua, Jesus, the Christ.

Silence permeated the room as many hugged and kissed the word with tearful delight and unhinged passion. Others randomly opened the pages and began reading verses. Pretty soon, the room was filled with various voices, all reading different verses, yet all somehow synchronizing in the same frequency.

One of the older members of the group said tearfully, "I recall when I had one of these books when I was younger but didn't have time to read it. Truth is, even though I was a Christian, I didn't care about it. Now it's the greatest treasure I could ever have. I'll never take it for granted again. Thank you."

Others nodded in tearful agreement. Charity added, "It's no accident that these were discovered on the same day the Inspectors planted the documents in our home and accused us of sedition. Because their focus was planting something false to later accuse us of, they missed the true treasure. God protected His Word, and will protect our loved ones, no matter the outcome. Truly, what the enemy had planned for evil, God turned it into good." (Genesis 50:20-21)

Everyone began praising God again as they held the Bibles in worship. When the praise and worship subsided, someone broke the silence and said, "We can't keep this to ourselves. We must share the Word throughout the Remnant community. But how can we share it when we're being watched?"

Another member answered, "If we each take certain books to copy, then we can get it done more quickly and spread the Word as they are completed."

"Copying is risky, and we can't leave any trackable or paper trail. We need another solution."

Kyly declared with excitement and much enthusiasm, "I know! We should memorize the Word and hide it in our hearts. It's what grandpa told mom. That way, we become living books and can share it wherever Abba leads us. And when we do, that person can also become living books by hiding the Word in their hearts as well and before you know it, everyone will become the Living Word. I'm sure that's what Abba would want. That way no one can ever take it away from us ever again."

"Out of the mouths of babes. I believe what Kyly just said is of God. I don't know about you, but I can't wait to devour what's in this book," responded another member of the group. "More than food and water, I crave to finally read this Word of God and never let it go. God will give us the grace to memorize and share it as He leads. I'm looking forward to becoming a Living Epistle as Kyly suggested. This is our only choice."

"What shall we do with the books after we memorize them?" another asked.

"I propose that we burn them. I believe God allowed us to discover them for such a time as this, (Esther 4:14) so that we can hide them in our hearts." Charity remarked. "Kyly is right. I will never forget my grandfather's last words. He prayed that we would know God and hide His Word in our heart. (Deuteronomy 6:6) I never understood what he meant. But now I do, this is the one true treasure that must be shared and cherished as long as God gives us breath."

The entire group, which was primarily composed of women and children, as their husbands were arrested by the GU, agreed on this strategy.

Over the course of the next forty days, they fasted, prayed and supernaturally memorized the Word as if their lives depended on it.

# CHAPTER 24

# DEPLORABLES

Delaying the trial to engage and incite the GU citizens against the accused traitors, the g.l.k. implemented a clever and divisive propaganda scheme. Knowing that communication was critical to ignite hatred in the masses to demand their execution, he depicted their possession of alleged seditious literature as deplorable, unpatriotic, treasonous, and mutinous. That, in addition to their premeditated, willful disobedience to participate in the coronation, they directly threatened the unity of the GU and every peaceful citizen.

Receiving daily communication inciting hate through divisive, manipulation and subliminal messaging, the masses, therefore, clamored for those arrested to be sentenced to death. Distorted pictures of rebellious prisoners showed them with gritted teeth, clenched fists, and fiery eyes. This, accompanied with cleverly fabricated quotes spewing their hatred of the GU were paraded on every news outlet. As sheep led to the slaughter, as the propaganda spread, so did the masses cry for the immediate and public execution of the deplorables. The GU sprang alive with the taste for blood and demanded their pound of flesh.

In contrast, pictures and communication from the g.l.k. portrayed a compassionate, just, understanding and forgiving global leader with the best interests of his flock in mind. Biding his time wisely, he waited until the demand for blood reached a climax and then, in a fatherly, slow, compassionate voice, Magor shared:

"Now is the time. I have heard your demand. Desiring mercy, compassion and forgiveness, I have deliberately not taken any action to date. But my love for you, my people, and my need to protect your peace of mind and your safety, I will grant your desires. We will stand together as one for justice and patriotism. The subversive actions of these deplorable individuals refusing to join in building a peaceful global union is beyond my comprehension. This leaves us no recourse but to rid our neatly ordered world (N.O.W.) of these vermin refusing to acknowledge me, us, and refusing to bow down to my position. We will fight together to cleanse our GU and establish our vision of peace, abundance, unity and true happiness for ourselves for generations to come."

In the empathetic tone, he continued, "I, therefore, commission you, my people, my life, my soul, to report to your local GU center any suspicious behavior you observe that contradicts this objective. You will be greatly rewarded and receive the National Heroic Award for your loyalty to the GU and to me, your g.l.k. Although I am not physically with you now, I hear your requests, I feel your need, and will grant the desires of your heart."

Those hearing the sincerity of his voice and believing he had their best interest at heart, bowed to him in worship, pride and admiration.

The following day, a guilty verdict was rendered. The execution date was set at the same time zone in each GU region. Steffen was one of the first thrown into the fiery pit.

On that same day, with tears rolling down their faces, his family burned the bibles. As the red smoke of the living epistles ascended, the Word, (John 1:1), the Lamb of God, seated at the right hand of the Father, (Mark 16:19) arose from His throne and extended His nail scarred hands. Seven stacks of individually sealed documents were placed in it. Looking to His Father, with tears streaming down His face, He lifted the first stack and began breaking open its red seal. (Revelation 6:1)

The day following the massacre, GU Inspectors conducted another random inspection. Finding nothing but grief stricken women and children at their targeted locations, they submitted a two word report, "Threats eliminated."

# CHAPTER 25

# G.I.P.P.

Wanting to ensure that the GU masses did not assume the identity of the region where they resided, they rotated random households every four years. Defining this process as the Global Identity Placement Plan (G.I.P.P.), it strategically disrupted families and friends. Under the pretense of equality for all, the G.I.P.P. was embraced by the citizens. Nonetheless, those living in the world, but who were not conformed to it, (Romans 12:2) welcomed the G.I.P.P. to spread the Gospel of Jesus Christ throughout the regions.

Outwardly appearing like any other GU citizen, they were inwardly living epistles of the Gospel. Led by the Holy Spirit, they lived and moved and had their being in the One true God; (Acts 17:28) Like Daniel and the three Hebrew boys in the Bible, (Daniel 1), although they lived in Babylon, many were placed in strategic leadership positions and lived among the citizens. Knowing there was something different about them, but unable to identify the difference, they were accepted by some and shunned by others. The Remnant, having received second sight, knew instinctively how to differentiate between those who had ears to hear and eyes to see the true and living God, from those choosing to walk in blindness to truth.

Therefore, walking by the Spirit of God, the Ecclesia, (also known as the Living Epistles, the Remnant), hidden in plain sight, boldly and courageous shared the gospel. Under the G.I.P.P. their missionary assignments were orchestrated by the GU. And as their collective body grew, so the Word of God spread until the numbers were to numerous to count.

Again, like the prophet Daniel in Babylon, the one thing that they would not do, was to bow down and worship or pray to any other god. Knowing this, the GU sought to infiltrate their borderless communities. Having failed through many strategies, they resorted to planting fictitious evidence and making false accusations. With only the power to kill the body, their propaganda could not deceive the heart. Therefore, infiltrating the Ecclesia proved to be an exercise in futility. Furthermore, pretenders were unable to deceive the Holy Spirit as their evil hearts were readily exposed. They either bowed their knees and surrendered their hearts to the One true and Living God, or mysteriously disappeared as quickly as they arrived, not being heard or seen again.

As with the early church, the Remnant multiplied daily, living each day as their last. Their mission was simple, to spread the Gospel and to glorify God. There was no place in their temporary existence on earth for denominational divide or differences in theology. They were citizens of the kingdom of heaven serving as temporary ambassadors on earth; (2 Corinthians 5:20) As such, they were not concerned with the things of this world. Committed to the Author and Finisher of their faith, (Hebrews 12:2) they lived a fearless life of unquestionable faith, absolute contentment and inexplicable peace, doing simple yet mighty exploits, (Daniel 11:32) in the only Name above all other names. (Philippians 2:9)

## CHAPTER 26

# NOW WHAT? - AGAIN

Discontented, bored, unhappy, and seeking continuous change, Magor hoped the next victory would produce the peace he desperately sought. Asking "Now What?" repeatedly, he paced like a trapped panther. Having exceeded all expectations, he contemplated his next conquest. Even though he was the mastermind of numerous world-changing inventions, there was one accomplishment that haunted him.

Like his grandfather, he wanted to not only invent, but to create. (Ref. R7:17, Dominion, The Beyond Limits Series, copyright 2020, W.A.Vega) And what he wanted to create was a new and improved humanity. The thought of fulfilling his grandfather's dream of evolving humankind to the next level seized his heart. Fire of determination burned within him as he visualized all possibilities. Unlike his grandfather's day, however, all resources were at his disposal. And who better than to experiment on but those who refused to worship him as their g.l.k.

Pretending to desire his cabinet's engagement in all GU affairs, he called an emergency meeting.

"Now that peace has been restored to the land," Romind stated, "The same question, 'Now What?' must be answered. Remember, we must give the illusion of engaging the masses in the administration of the GU. If I'm asking the question, I'm sure they must be too. And that's what we need to discuss today. What is our "Now What?" answer."

Zukorain Sedski replied, "I've been thinking the very same thing as it's been reported that there's some unrest with the citizens since the public execution of the deplorables four months ago. I have a suggestion. Your coronation truly unified us. What if we had another celebratory event? This time a wedding. We briefly discussed this some time ago, but the timing was not right."

"A wedding?" questioned Ezari Nuka trying to discredit Zukorain, "Not that again. I thought we already dismissed that idea?"

"Are you suggesting again that I should marry?" Magor rudely intervened. "I still find the thought repulsive. That's the last thing I need. Besides, I was the one who abolished it. Why would I want to be strapped to anyone? I can have anyone at any time for any reason. What benefits does it offer me? Or the GU for that matter? Thanks for suggesting it, but I have no interest and still don't see its purpose. Besides, I have something else in mind. But let's explore it a second time before dismissing the thought. I need to fully understand the benefits to me personally and the GU. I'm intrigued as to why this subject is being presented again. Lucky for you, I am patient and an open book. And above all else, I want what's best for my subjects."

Seizing the opportunity, Zukorain presented his proposal, "It's time to celebrate and unify the GU again and what better occasion than to have a royal wedding? The last ten plus years have been hell on earth. We've achieved a great deal to get to this point. Now that the storms have passed and we've silenced all known and unknown forces, it's time to celebrate. We've earned it and the people need it. It will unite us even more. And as the g.l.k., you will be the only one in the GU who can have global brides, demonstrating that you're above your own law. You will stand apart, towering over everyone else. You alone are the g.l.k. Besides, this will be the perfect occasion for global worship that will once again expose our enemies."

"Umm," replied Magor. "Suddenly this idea is beginning to sound appealing. Now that we have control, we can loosen the reigns a bit. Not only will this call for celebration, it will seal our identity as one GU." Thinking inwardly of his primary motive, he said aloud, "I also see the opportunity for global worship that is sure to expose more of those deplorable dissenters who still refuse to bow to me. I smell blood and see another bonfire on the horizon."

Taking time to digest the thought, he further added, "Ah, now I see the value of a royal wedding. But there's the question of who would I marry?"

Noticing a hush in the room, he continued answering his own question, "I want a suitable person from each geographic region chosen as a representative and we will formalize our relationship with this royal wedding. Let's make it a contest and you can choose the final four, from the east, west, north and south. In fact, let's create a harem of brides and through my union with them, it will be the same as choosing everyone in my kingdom as my bride. That's the only way to ensure absolute loyalty going forward, and even though I believe I will live forever, I want to preserve my royal line in perpetuity."

Everyone arose from the table applauding his decision, and then bowing low before him declared in union, "You are our g.l.k., now and forever."

Capitalizing on the moment, Magor arose and said, "Great, I now understand how important this union will be to maintain peace and unity within our kingdom. Make no mistake, whatever I do, is to secure my reign. Remember, I am not flesh and blood as any ordinary being. I am the people's g.l.k. They need my protection and I will always secure their peace and wellbeing. Nonetheless, so that the natives don't get too restless and begin thinking on their own, we need to carefully plan our next steps and how we will engage them in the process. They must see this wedding as a true union of souls. I'll leave the details in your hands and expect a carefully crafted communication plan within the next week, beginning with the global contest and choosing the four brides. Let's make this the grandest event of the age, even more glorious than my coronation. Yes, this will be a global wedding, a royal celebration in which everyone is invited."

Dismissing his cabinet, he told Zukorain to remain behind to discuss something privately. Puffed up with pride that his g.l.k. would want his personal opinion on another matter, Zukorain nodded in reply, "As you wish my g.l.k." A few minutes later, Magor walked away, thinking to himself, *While the world is distracted with this wedding, I can focus on my experiment. What better way to ensure I have all the resources I will need for my next creation. I will evolve humankind to the next level. I will succeed where my grandfather failed. Everyone will know that I am truly god, lord and king, with the power of my will to create.*

The following week, his cabinet presented a plan they believed would not only further unite the GU, but also expose traitors among them.

## CHAPTER 27

# RESPONDERS

According to the plan, a global call for potential brides was made. Requirements were very broad yet specific; anyone between the ages of fifteen and thirty-five were eligible candidates. Gender was not a consideration since the world was declared a unisex entity in the prior generation. However, included in the fine print, those selected must be willing to leave their home and families and live solely within the g.l.k's domain. This included the four representative brides, and all others selected to be part of the g.l.k.'s bridal entourage. His harem.

Despite the broad and ambiguous terms of the plan, candidate profiles began flooding in. The privilege to live in close proximity to the g.l.k. was considered an opportunity not to be refused. The selection committee, comprised of the g.l.k.'s cabinet members, ensured the one requirement Magor insisted on, was that the selected female candidates must be at the peak of their child-bearing age.

Profiles that made it through the first round were split equally from the east, west, north and south regions. Unknown to the candidates, this marriage was purely political and represented the union the g.l.k. desired to have with all his subjects. And although four individuals would be selected, the majority of the applicants who met the g.l.k.'s qualifications would also be selected to be part of his harem, both males and females.

Fervently praying for guidance, the Remnant questioned whether they should engage in this process. Many believed that it would be advantageous to infiltrate the palace with living epistles, while others believed it to be a suicide mission. As they prayed, the Holy Spirit highlighted the history of Sampson (Judges 13-16) and Queen Esther, (Book of Esther) both Israelites who intentionally gained access to the enemy's camp to achieve God's purposes.

Sensing the possibilities and guided by the Holy Spirit, the unanimous decision was to submit as many profiles of eligible brides from each region as possible. To their delight, numerous profiles were selected for the second phase of the selection process. This included a face-to-face interview with the selection committee. Knowing the risks involved if their true identity were discovered, the Living Epistles blended in with the other GU citizens without compromising their beliefs.

While seizing every opportunity to reflect the true and only God, Lord and King of kings, they focused on their mission as representatives of their Kingdom. Many were selected for the second round of interviews. Then one, Dr. Jael Debor, (known as Dr. Jael), who was neither a believer nor unbeliever, was the last to be selected as one of the final four. Unknown to the g.l.k., his palace was about to be saturated with living epistles within and outside its walls.

# CHAPTER 28

# DR. JAEL

Jael Debor was as intelligent as she was beautiful. Born within the GU structure, she received the trackable nanochip at birth and from all external appearances was part of the system. Receiving her doctorate in medical science and obstetrics in her twenties, she became one of the youngest doctors to make medical history. Her reputation for attempting the impossible, especially that of saving the life of the unborn while still in the womb, was becoming legendary.

Bold, courageous and fearless, she passionately pursued her one fascination, human life. She, therefore, sought to understand how it was created, how it developed and what occurred at death. A firm believer in science, there was one foundational truth she wrestled with, that nothing cannot create something. Believing the cause and effect theory, she sought answers to understand the intricate design of the human body and was determined to know the designer.

Reaching the conclusion that the human body and all creation were not triggered by an accidental sudden explosion from an inexplicable force, but a well-designed plan by a being infinitely greater and more intelligent than humankind, she sought answers. Her obsession with scientific research led her to the only conclusion she could logically reach. There must be a more intelligent, uncreated being with the mastermind to design and sustain all that it created. She, therefore, sought answers in creation itself. Not finding any sound answers, she started looking outside creation and began entertaining the possibility of an uncreated, omnipotent, eternal, creator, God of all.

Wanting to validate her theory, she became obsessed with the g.l.k., Magor G. Romind. Was he merely a man like all others, or a higher being? Therefore, when the invitation to apply to be one of his brides was presented, she seized it.

Taking a quick nap in her office following a long and extremely risky surgery, she heard an inner voice say, "I AM your Creator. I AM the breath of life." Awaking and looking around to find the source of the voice, she concluded that it was just her imagination. Moments later, she heard the voice repeating the same statement. This time, she quietly asked, "Who are you?" before returning to sleep.

Within minutes, there was a knock at her door. Arising to open it, a nurse, dressed in white linen, stood before her and said, "I was told to let you know that the Creator is the I AM that I AM. He is the One you have been seeking. His name is Wonderful and He is the One and only true and living uncreated, Creator God."

Staring in amazement, Dr. Jael asked, "Did you also hear the voice? Is that why you came to speak to me? How can I meet this uncreated, Creator? Where can I find Him?"

The nurse replied, "Keep seeking and you shall find Him. You shall see Him with the eyes of your heart. Do you believe?"

Quickly responding, she said, "Yes, I believe, but I need to know more."

A colleague walking by saw Dr. Jael standing at her office door talking, but no one was there. Curious, he stopped and asked, "Is everything okay?"

She responded, "Why do you ask? I was talking to the nurse who knocked on my door. Didn't you see him?"

"No, I didn't see anyone," her colleague answered. "But I know you just completed a long and exhausting surgery. You must be tired. Congratulations by the way. Both patients are doing well. Now get some rest."

Looking quizzically at him, she returned to the sofa and fell soundly asleep. When she awoke, the words and the interaction with the mysterious nurse burned within her. She knew that the voice and brief conversation was real but didn't know how to interpret it.

Later that week, following another surgery, she heard the same voice, repeating the same words. The following day, she received a response from the g.l.k.'s bridal selection committee congratulating her on her selection as one of his brides.

# CHAPTER 29

# APATHETIC GROOM

"Let's get this over with. The sooner the better. I've got more important things to do," Magor groaned with impatience. Dressed in his familiar royal robes, he adorned the appearance of a regal king waiting to unite with his beloved queen.

Taking one last glance in the mirror, he said, "Good enough for me. It's the brides that should be anxious about their appearance right now, because if I don't approve of any of them, there will be consequences."

His closest cabinet member and friend, Zukorain, replied, "I'm sure your g.l.k., that you will be pleased with all of our selections. Each one represents a region. Besides, this is a political marriage in name only. They get nothing out of this but the opportunity to reside in your kingdom and make an occasional appearance at your command."

"Is everything else prepared as discussed?" Magor inquired. "I need to make sure everything goes as planned. This is not just an ordinary wedding, it's my ascension to infamy. I shall be in a category all to myself. No one will doubt that I am the one and only g.l.k. of all time. And in case you forget, the consequences of any mishaps are life changing for you, your family and everyone involved."

Nodding in agreement, Zukorain bowed his head and replied, "Everything will go as planned, your g.l.k."

Then taking his royal staff in hand and placing his elaborate crown on his head, he marched out of the room, with attendants lifting the train of his robe as he went.

As with his coronation, the event was broadcasted live throughout the union while the actual event was held in the Western Region C.O.S.E (Center Of Self-Enlightenment). With the brides identity a closely guarded secret, even from the g.l.k., the streets were lined with anxious masses vying for their first glimpse of the groom and his brides. At first glance of his entourage, cheers and shouts exploded with frenzied passion and admiration that continued increasing in volume. Then a loud chant broke through, "We love our bridegroom g.l.k. We love our bridegroom g.l.k."

Everyone in physical attendance and those watching virtually, picked up the melody as the shout escalated in passion and unified hysteria. As his carrier reached the entrance to the C.O.S.E., he ceremoniously turned around and sent kisses into the feverish crowd. Many swooned in delight and some even fainted, overwhelmed by his regal appearance.

Capitalizing on the moment, Magor removed his crown, and waved it before the masses and said through a microphone, "You are all my bride. My vow is to you, my beloved people, my pride and joy. Today we will be wed."

Inconspicuously yawning, he turned around and entered the C.O.S.E. and waited for the brides' arrival.

CHAPTER 30

# SMOKE & MIRRORS

Following closely behind the groom's entrance, the four selected brides dismounted from their carriages. Each wearing the same bridal attire that included a shimmering white outer tunic, trimmed in a wide layer of glittering gold border, and a purple sash draped diagonally across their shoulder displaying the name of the region they represented. There were two biological males and two biological females. They were all similar in height, weight and age. Following their groom's example, they paused before entering the C.O.S.E. The people again exploded in applause while dancing and chanting with chaotic delight, "We are his bride; we are his bride; we are his bride."

Caught up in the moment, three of the representative brides also began chanting although they were instructed to remain silent. As they chanted, the people became a wild mob storming towards the C.O.S.E. Instantly, as if waiting on standby, the silver locust appeared and formed a barricade around the building completely shielding it from the turbulent mob. Seeing the shield, the masses retreated and returned to their designated places. All but one slid unnoticed inside the reception area of the outer sanctuary and hid unnoticed behind a life sized statue of its founder, William T. Surrogate.

After the brides entered, the heavy steel doors shut behind them. The anticipated ceremony of the century was about to begin. Carefully following instructions, the brides walked alone down the long middle isle. Reaching the front of the platform, they took their designated places at a kneeling stool that had the name of their region clearly displayed. With their heads bowed, the groom approached on the platform. Without looking at them, he stood and declared:

"Today you, as a representative of your region, and representing the entire GU, are voluntarily uniting with me, soul and spirit. As my bride, do you promise to serve, obey, and give your complete allegiance to me as your g.l.k and husband?"

As if on cue, with their heads still bowed, all the brides but one responded in unison, "Yes, we do." The audience within the C.O.S.E. and many attending virtually also responded.

Caught up in the moment and more focused on the camera and his audience, Magor didn't notice that one did not respond. Continuing his questioning, he asked, "Do you promise to bow and worship me, as your g.l.k and husband?" he continued.

Still unnoticed, all but one replied the same as with the first question, "Yes, we do."

The questioning continued, "Do you promise to lay down your life in any capacity as needed by your g.l.k and husband?"

Again, all but one replied in unison, "Yes, we do."

Then looking straight into the cameras, he responded with a deliberate pause after each word, "Then, I, your g.l.k, Magor G. Romind, take each of you, from the North, the South, the East and the West, as a representative of my global bride." He then placed a golden bracelet in their hands and continued, "Arise, my brides. Take your position to partner with me as we defend our union against all enemies, seen or unseen. We will build together. We will evolve together. We will conquer together. We will laugh together. Not even death will tear us apart. Now let's celebrate as never before."

When he finished his declaration, those listening within the C.O.S.E. and those virtually attending, again exploded in applause, shouting and dancing. Balloon, confetti, and fireworks blasted a sound as that of a thousand cannons. The festivities began as the g.l.k. led his representative brides out the building. Just as he walked through the reception area, and began entering the outer court, a figure emerged from the background. In a flash, the figure appeared to pierce a sharp carving knife into the g.l.k.'s heart and disappeared among the crowd. Blood spattered everywhere as the brides' faces and crisp white clothes were covered in red.

In that moment, the celebration turned to shock and silence. Then amidst loud cries of anguish someone yelled, "The g.l.k. is dead." Stunned, Dr. Jael, who was walking directly behind him, looked intently at the still figure of the g.l.k. lying in what appeared to be a pool of blood. Being familiar with the look, feel and smell of blood and death, she became suspicious.

However, just as she was about to lean in closer to examine the body, she was rudely shoved aside.

CHAPTER 31

# DELUSION

Mourning transitioned to anger, then to rage, as news of the g.l.k.'s death ravished the citizens hearts. The perpetrator(s) had to be found and publicly punished. Anyone presumed to be anti-GU in word or deed were suspect. In despondence, mobs took to the streets and began lashing out at anyone and anything in their way. The hope of the GU was dead, and there was no vision apart from him.

His second in command, Zukorain Sedski, as if prepared for this moment, immediately took center stage and declared, "Words cannot describe the pain and anguish we're all experiencing. G.l.k. Magor G. Romind was, and still is a great man. I say 'still is' because we don't believe that even death can conquer him. He will always be alive to us. He would want us to continue his legacy of peace and plan for a future filled with hope for better days ahead. How like him to give up his life for his brides. It is no accident that this would occur on our wedding day. For it was a royal wedding between us and our beloved g.l.k. So, let's make him proud by following in his footsteps and secure his legacy for eternity. We will find the perpetrators of this heinous crime and they will be punished. We've already identified several whom we believe may have committed this national crime against us, against humanity, against hope and peace."

Continuing, he orated, "In the meantime, let us return to peace and hope. Even though his body may be dead, he is alive and will always live in our hearts. As soon as we complete all forensic examinations, and his body is released, it will be laid in state and viewable at any time via our virtual viewing system. Details of our progress and future plans will be shared as they are developed. I am sure the g.l.k. will thank you for your tears and continued commitment to him during these transitionary days. He is worthy of your praise and worship now more than ever. On behalf of the g.l.k., thank you."

Cloaked in grief, the citizens were momentarily comforted and waited anxiously for the next steps.

CHAPTER 32

# THEATRICS

The GU watched and mourned as the body of their beloved g.l.k. rested in state under the 24/7 virtual viewing system of the C.O.S.E. On the sixth day following his death, the body appeared to move. Captivated by this natural impossibility, those watching thought their eyes had deceived them. As they watched, the body that laid prostrate for the past six days, suddenly began arising from the platform where it was laid. A global hush descended on the earth as everyone held their breath believing yet questioning what they were seeing. Nonetheless, the facts seemed undeniable.

Appearing before the camera, Zukorain Sedski rushed to the g.l.k. and bowed before him stating, "I knew you wouldn't leave us." Quickly ascending the steps leading to the platform, a doctor assisted Magor, and they descended.

As if in stunned surprise himself, Magor declared before the camera, "I don't know what happened, but I know that I was dead, and now I am alive. Now the entire world knows that I am not a mere mortal. Humanity can indeed evolve to a higher life form. I am your god, lord and king."

The camera then went blank as everyone watching held their breath in hushed awe. When the cameras resumed recording, it showed Magor surrounded by doctors examining him. His shirt was unbuttoned revealing a perfectly healed chest without a trace of the puncture wound from where the knife appeared to have penetrated his heart.

After the examination, the lead physician declared, "This is indeed a miracle. We all saw the stabbing six days ago and know that our g.l.k. was dead. Now he is fully alive and well as if there was never any trauma to his body. There is no medical evidence to explain what took place. All we, as scientists can say, is that he was dead, and is now alive. He deserves our praise and worship."

News of the g.l.k.'s immortality spread instantly throughout the globe. Many who doubted that he was the g.l.k., believed. Even many of the elect Remnant believed and shifted their faith. Those who believed now posed a threat to the true Remnant who counted their lives as loss for the sake of the gospel of Jesus, Christ. (Philippians 3:8-10)

CHAPTER 33

# DEBRIS

"This has been one of the longest weeks of my life," declared Magor to his trusted cabinet member, Zukorain. "Hiding in the bunker was no fun. But it did give me the quiet time to make improvements to my next invention. And I now know that I can trust you with my life. You will be greatly rewarded."

"Thank you my g.l.k. I am committed to serving you with my life," he replied with much pomposity.

"I would like to have a special dinner to honor you and everyone else who was involved in planning and executing this week's event," Magor stated. "Everything went flawlessly and achieved its purpose. Now everyone will honor and fear me as their g.l.k., of that I have no doubt. But this is just a beginning. We've got much work to do."

Wanting to review the events, Zukorain responded, "Yes, there are a few individuals who played a major part in this week's success that we especially need to honor."

Much to Magor's distaste, he continued rambling on, "The man who stabbed you was perfect. While everyone saw him, it was so quick, and there was so much blood that no one can recall what he looked like. I didn't know the bag contained that much. It looked real and spewed out so rapidly. Everyone was shocked. Not to mention your part in the event."

Ignoring Magor's disapproving glare, he laughed hilariously and continued, "You also played the perfect role. No one, other than the few of us suspected anything but a real stabbing and your subsequent death. It was ingenious! Yes, let's privately celebrate our success. Your reign is secure."

Despising his loquaciousness, Magor responded, "Let's get everyone together privately this week, tomorrow even. I can't wait to give each of you what you deserve."

Arriving with eager anticipation of being rewarded by the g.l.k., were six individuals, including his friend, Zukorain. All had participated in the subterfuge of the stabbing and subsequent events. Joining Magor for dinner and a private celebration, they envisioned rewards of promotion, status, power, and prosperity.

The table was elaborately set with the best of all wines and other drinks, exotic appetizers and elaborate food choices. Overcome with the generosity of the g.l.k., the guests indulged themselves to their heart's desire. Just before dinner was served, Magor arrived.

Taking his position at the head of the table, he said, "I want to thank you all for your excellent service and loyalty to me. This has been a tough week for all of us and our citizens. Notwithstanding the challenges and risks involved in what was accomplished, you served me well. And for that you will be well rewarded. However, I want to ensure that you maintain confidentiality as previously agreed. I trusted you with an enormous task and need to know that you can be trusted as well. Let's drink and celebrate our success."

Everyone around the table responded with assurance that they did not share any information about their role in the stabbing. The two individuals who doubled for the g.l.k., and pretended to be dead during the six days, added, "It was a pleasure to double as you, my grace. It was also an honor to die as you."

The room broke out in drunken laughter as others joined in with similar comments as they recounted the week's events. Just before dinner was served, Magor said, "I've reserved the best for last. My special, private collection of a rare wine that's made for my table only. Let's toast to our success."

Pride imploded the hearts of the guests who were amazed that they were sitting at the g.l.k's table, drinking wine from his private collection, and being honored. They eagerly lifted their wine glasses and toasted to their success. Many guzzled the wine as gluttonous fools and within minutes, they were gagging and writhing on the floor in agony as life seeped from their lungs. Magor stood over them and sneered, "Now I know the secret is safe," and walked away.

Summoning two titanium snakes programmed to remove debris, he left the room triumphant and began preparing for his next State of the Union address.

CHAPTER 34

# ILLUSIONS

The following day, Magor, arrayed in his royal attire, stood before the camera as he addressed the Global Union. In his most fatherly, tone, and seemingly on the brink of tears, he began by saying, "My beloved, we have endured one of the most excruciating weeks of our existence. Enemies of the Union thought they could rob us of the exhilaration of our marriage and our future together by their attempt to destroy me and annihilate our Union. Thinking they had killed my body, they proved beyond doubt my immortality. Now we know that death itself cannot extinguish this flame. I am here now. I am here to stay and lead you, my beloved people, into a magnificent future. You gave me the hope and strength to defy death. You are the reason I can stand before you today, without even a scar to remind us of the evil perpetrated against us."

Slowly pulling aside his robe and inner garment, he exposed his chest and continued with his voice increasing in volume, "As you can see, there is no scar." Allowing his garments to fall back into place, he proceeded, his tone increasing in conviction and strength, "In fact, while they intended to strike a lethal blow to my heart, the heart of our Union, we have struck a lethal blow against them. I am pleased to let you know that we have identified the nest of vipers who executed this crime and have already destroyed them. Their names and faces will not be remembered in history for we have erased them from our midst as if they never existed. So, if you know someone who has mysteriously disappeared don't be concerned. Ask no questions. Cast no shadow that may imply that you may have also been complicit in their heinous crimes. Simply assume that their disappearance is no accident and a gift to our Union"

Looking boldly into the camera, he further declared, "I serve notice on anyone, or any group who attempt the same to me or my people. Similar, swift judgement and punishment will come upon you. We shall always win in any opposition against us. Victory is, and always will be ours. So, let us celebrate. We still have a wedding feast to celebrate victory. Let the festivities begin as we usher in this new season of development in our union."

When he concluded his address, the sky exploded with fireworks. The silver locusts above appeared to be dancing beneath the clouds. The titanium snakes shifted below the earth and the world momentarily danced in response. Even the ocean danced, as the steel-like fish began flying over the surface of the deep releasing an iridescent glow that reflected on the water. Citizens of the GU began celebrating with abandon for the next seven weeks, openly indulging in anything their hearts desired.

In the meantime, Magor patted himself on the back and thought, *Such gullible fools. I need a higher species of humanity to serve me. Now that everyone knows I am untouchable and unquestionable, I can begin creating and finish what my grandfather began.*

Before finishing his thought, the true King of kings, the Lamb of God broke the first seal and opened a legal document. "… and behold, a white horse. He who sat on it had a bow; and a crown was given to him, and he went out conquering and to conquer." (Revelation 6:2)

The mystery of the fullness of lawlessness was bulging as a woman in the last stages of pregnancy. Birth pangs began. Now was the time for the Remnant to step out of the shadows and own their destiny as kings, priests and prophets in a wicked and perverse generation.

# PART THREE

# WON

. . .

# CHAPTER 35

# SILVER RAIN

With the first seal broken, the one mounted on the white horse raced swiftly through the atmosphere releasing thunder, rain, hail, and lightening as he went. The speed and power of his gallop shook the skies and rattled the silver locusts as a paper kite in a tropical storm. In a moment, hundreds of thousands of the silver locusts imploded releasing chunks of hot silver to the earth. Wherever it landed and whomever it touched other than the Remnant, were instantly burned to ashes. On that one day, thousands died.

The fragile peace of the GU was rattled. Responding quickly to settle the masses, the GU office of Meteorology reported, "Urgent, it has been reported that it's raining silver in various locations. While we investigate its source, all citizens are urged not to go near or touch the debris. We believe this to be a hostile attack against us by unseen forces. Rest assured that our g.l.k. will protect you and we will fight."

Assembling his cabinet, the g.l.k. stated, "There is obviously a malfunction in the locust hardware or this breech would not have occurred. While we strengthen this weakness in the design, we need to strategically attribute these deaths to 'acts of god,' and the people who still follow this fictitious notion. I want your plan tomorrow on how we should proceed on our counter-attack. I'm focused on another project at this time and don't have the time, energy or effort to engage in this one. Let's make sure that for every death of a loyal GU citizen, we eliminate at least two deplorables, including women and children. Let's send them a threatening message that no one is safe. That no one can protect them from me. Is that clear?"

Since Zukorain Sedski's sudden disappearance, the remaining cabinet members were gripped with even more fear and intimidation by the g.l.k.'s unpredictable abuse of power. Ezari Nuka, however, took the initiative to respond, "It's very clear your g.l.k. and you will have our plan tomorrow. I want to remind you that we never addressed those who did not attend our wedding nor bowed down in worship. With the GU in mourning over your pronounced death, we did not follow-up, but now may be the right time to do so."

"I completely forgot that we never followed through on that opportunity. That's a good starting point," Magor responded. "Send me your report in the morning and I want swift action."

As he spoke, the One holding the sealed documents broke the second seal, "…and another horse, fiery red, went out. And it was granted to the one who sat on it to take peace from the earth, and that people should kill one another; and there was given to him a great sword." (Revelation 6:4)

CHAPTER 36

# BITING SNAKES

The following night, before the diabolical plan was sent to the g.l.k., the titanium snakes patrolling the earth beneath, detected a threat above ground. Programmed to instantly respond, they emerged and began biting anyone in sight. The puncture wound released a poison that invaded the brain causing momentary madness. In a frenzy of disorientation, people began attacking each other, killing themselves and others, even those in the same household. Whatever peace remained disintegrated in a wave of uncontrollable carnage. Hundreds of thousands were killed before the software was reprogrammed and the slaughter ended.

Hoping to assuage the masses and restore their neatly ordered world, the GU office of Meteorology reported, "We are aware of another attack by unseen forces that causes temporary insanity and rage by usually peaceful, harmless, innocent people to destroy each other. This is nothing but a vicious assault on humanity. Undoubtedly another 'act of god.' We assure you that we have eliminated the threat and the spread of this poison among us. Do not fear. We are in control and will launch an attack sending a clear message that we are the master of our own fate and will bow to no other god than our beloved g.l.k."

Before the last sentence was spoken, the third seal was opened, and "...a black horse, and he who sat on it had a pair of scales in his hand. And I heard a voice in the midst of the four living creatures saying, 'A quart of wheat for a denarius, and three quarts of barley for a denarius; and do not harm the oil and the wine.'" (Revelation 6:6)

The titanium snakes, having released their venom upon the earth, destroyed the wheat, the barley and all the earth's food, causing a global food shortage. Prices soared. Supplies dwindled. Famine ensued and people, gripped by pandemonium, trampled each other to secure their next meal.

In the midst of this swirl, the fourth seal was opened and "...a pale horse...And the name of him who sat on it was Death, and Hades followed with him. And power was given to them over a fourth of the earth, to kill with the sword with hunger, with death, and by beasts of the earth." (Revelation 6:8)

# CHAPTER 37

# PROPS & PROPAGANDA

Caught off guard by this chain of events, Magor carefully crafted his communication and made an impromptu address to the GU:

"Unbelievable. Simply unbelievable. That we have been attacked for no apparent reason by evil, diabolical, unseen forces. Notwithstanding, we shall prevail. We own our destinies. We will never give up. Our enemies have used our defense systems against us. Traitors and unconscionable mass murders, that's who they are. And they will pay the price for their seditious treachery," he seethed.

He drank in a breath, paused for a moment and then vehemently declared, "We have already identified the names and locations of those involved in this crime against humanity, one they have done in the name of their diabolical god. I serve notice on you today. We know who you are and we are coming after you. We will spare no mercy as you have not spared any on us. I also make this appeal to you, my beloved GU citizens, we will stop at nothing to protect your interests and secure our future. Have no fear. We shall prevail."

Before he finished his speech, the steel-like metallic fish, mysteriously malfunctioned and launched an attack on the earth. Many who were not killed by burning debris falling from the silver locust above, or by the poison and famine caused by the  titanium snakes below, were suddenly struck down by the gigantic beasts that primarily roamed the seas, the land and the air. When it was over, the death toll was over a fourth of the earth. (Revelation 6:8) There were still three seals left to be opened. No man, woman or child was safe, except those covered with the blood of the Lamb, whose names were written in the Lamb's Book of Life.

Sensing his time running out, Magor sent an urgent note to his cabinet to execute the names on the list. They were to ask one question, "Will you bow down and worship the g.l.k.?" Those refusing were to be bound and thrown into a burning fire. Those who did bow, were also to be publicly burned for their cowardice and questionable loyalty. Not suspecting that there would be any deplorables in his own household, they were automatically exempt from the list. The following day, a great many were executed for their faith, along with many more who were executed for their cowardice. Charity Marble, her son Callem, and daughter Kyly, were among them.

Following their execution, the g.l.k. announced a great celebration and declared triumph over their enemies. While the smoke of the persecuted saints ascended into heaven, the people danced in the streets over their ashes. The fifth seal was opened.

# CHAPTER 38

# THE FIFTH SEAL

"When He opened the fifth seal, I saw under the altar the souls of those who had been slain for the word of God and for the testimony which they held. And they cried with a loud voice, saying, "How long, O Lord holy and true, until You judge and avenge our blood on those who dwell on the earth? Then a white robe was given to each of them; and it was said to them that they should rest a little while longer, until both the number of their fellow servants and their brethren, who would be killed as they were, was completed." (Revelation 6:9-10)

The persecuted saints, covered in white robes, rested in abundant peace. In the meantime, the mystery of lawlessness on earth rose to its peak. The GU became a drunk and disorderly world where self-pleasure and self-worship manifested in indescribable behaviors. The deepest darkness prevailed. In the midst of this season, Magor, vowing to complete the work his great grandfather initiated, began what he believed would be his greatest invention, re-creating humankind.

Believing that nothing was impossible, he determined to evolve humanity to a higher level. Now, more than ever, this new breed of humanity was needed. They were his path to surpassing greatness and immeasurable glory which his soul yearned for daily. With his unquestionable power and authority, he established a fetal re-engineering research center. Wanting to honor his father's lifelong hero, he named it the Nimrod-Romind Research Institute (NRRI). Beginning with improving the nanochip he developed for the silver locust, the titanium snakes and the steel-like fish, he was ready to start the next phase of his research.

However, to do so required expertise in embryonic re-engineering and fetal development. With all resources at his disposal, he summoned Dr. George Raclivio, a renowned physician and personal acquaintance. Eagerly arriving at the NRRI, Dr. Raclivio sat in shocked silence as Magor shared his vision of evolving humanity to a new level and the role he wanted him to play in the experiments. The more Magor shared, the more Dr. Raclivio was convinced of his insanity. However, fearing for his life, he responded, "I see the possibilities but I cannot do this alone. I will need at least one other doctor with similar expertise to assist. In fact, there is one colleague I will need to partner with and I believe she is here, in your palace as one of your four regional brides, Dr. Jael."

Without giving it a second thought, Magor replied, "Consider it done. I will summon her. Whatever resources you need are at your disposal. I have perfected the nanochip, your job is to implant it during the early stages of embryonic development so that it assimilates with the brain and modifies all motor skills. I already have many seeds marinating in test tubes ripe for transference into the womb. Let's begin, time is running out."

Stunned by the summons, Dr. Jael walked into the NRRI and met the g.l.k. for the first time since she arrived at his palace. Her first impression was that he was much smaller and older than he appeared publicly. He was thin and gaunt, with cold, unemotional eyes that rarely looked up.

Intimately familiar with the human body, she listened in shocked silence and awe as he described his vision. Thinking to herself, *'This little man is mad. He's no more a higher being than the least of us. He must be stopped.'* She looked at her colleague, whose eyes conveyed the same thought, and replied, "I see and will do everything I can to advance life. When do we begin?"

Hearing what he wanted to hear, Magor enthusiastically responded, "We can start today. We have rooms prepared for you in the lab. Of course, we expect you both to live on site to be available at all times. I plan to be personally involved in every step of this process and will spend the majority of my time in the lab as well. Jael, I will let our staff know to move you there right away. George, there's no need for you to leave. We've already made your arrangements. As you can surmise, this research is highly confidential and must not be shared with anyone, including the subjects. Is that clear?"

Believing he was unstable, but knowing he was the most powerful man on earth, they nodded. Magor then stated, "I will give you a quick tour of the lab and then someone will escort you to your respective offices and living suites. We will officially begin tomorrow."

Later that night, Dr. Jael was awakened by a familiar voice whispering in her ear, "I have brought you here 'for such a time as this.' (Esther 4:14). You will know what to do."

Responding to the voice, she asked, "Who are you? And what will I know to do?"

With the words spoken leaving an indelible record in her soul, she returned to a restless sleep.

CHAPTER 39

# THE NRRI

While the GU citizens were being ravaged by the pandemic, famine, poverty, plagues and death, Magor was building a lavish state of the art research institute. Complete with AI, (Artificial Intelligence), robotic intelligence equipment, and the highest level of security surveillance available, he spared no expense. The Nimrod-Romind Research Institute (NRRI) was more of an impenetrable fort than any other entity in the GU. Access in and out of the NRRI was tightly controlled and monitored by the silver locusts patrolling above the ceiling and the titanium snakes below the flooring. Preferring to trust AI rather than man, there were large, fish-like figures posted at each entrance and exit on 24/7 guard. Audio and visual equipment recorded every sound and movement. And Magor controlled them all with a small remote control masquerading as an innocuous silver clasp on his belt.

This fort-like structure had many faux windows. Each faux window had an external monitor attached to it that provided a virtual view from a range of programmable landscapes. With the sun, moon and stars in constellations, it was set as a light source at designated times.

Additionally, there was a 24/7 cafeteria manned by AI robots that prepared and served meals on demand from meats, grains and vegetables raised and grown within the palace grounds. Everything was controlled, including a private water supply from a hidden reservoir on the property. There was a faux indoor beach area complete with sun and sand, as well as an internal gym to ensure all guests had access indoors to everything otherwise available outdoors.

As in his great grandfather's day, the NRRI had several rooms with hundreds of beds lined against a wall. Each bed had AI monitors embedded to a clear protective screen that separated the beds from each other. With built in sensors to track movement, including movement within the womb, nothing was private.

In this self-sustaining building, once a person entered, they couldn't leave without being granted access. However, despite the luxurious appearance of a vacation resort, it felt and looked like a prison. And being a keen observer of her surroundings, Dr. Jael made a mental note of every detail during their tour. The one thing that eluded her, however, was how the building was monitored, and where Magor kept the master key.

# CHAPTER 40

# SPECIMENS

Eager to begin the experiment, Magor shared with the women who were strategically placed in his harem for such a time as this, "All of you were selected as my global bride to partner with me for a higher calling. Thank you in advance for your willing participation in a life-changing research. You will go down in history as pioneers, enthusiastic to sacrifice your future for the sake of advancing humankind. Your children and grandchildren, future generations will honor your names and your decision to lay down your life for their sakes. Thank you. Today you will be transferred to the Nimrod-Romind Research Institute, (NRRI). It will be your new home, even more luxurious than what you have enjoyed here in the palace. Without going into detail, I assure you that everything you need will be provided for. All we ask is that you relax and pretend that you are going away for an extended period of rest and pampering in a new location. As we have done in the past, we will take care of everything. You already know that you can trust me. I will do nothing to harm you. My only interest, is in making you and humankind better, stronger, more versatile, equipped for anything and any environment, perhaps even defying death."

Many received his message with great expectation, but many, who were intentionally placed there as vessels of honor about the Father's business, received the Word with immense skepticism. Knowing there was a battle ahead, they prayed inwardly for wisdom and guidance on how to spread the good news of the gospel of Jesus Christ...for how to be the fragrance of Christ to those who are perishing. (2 Corinthians 2:15). Knowing the end from the beginning, they trusted in the unseen hand of their loving God, fully persuaded that He causes all things to work together for good to those who love Him and are called according to His purposes. (Romans 8:28)

As beds in the NRRI began filling with specimens tricked into what they thought would be a life of ease living in the g.l.k.'s, harem, they now found themselves to be prisoners. However, to the g.l.k., they were bodies to be exploited as a means to his end. Now as captives in the NRRI, they realized that they involuntarily offered their bodies as living sacrifices to be experimented on. Seeking hope, they eagerly listened to the ones who always seemed to have words of life and hope. Many, therefore, put their faith in the God of hope and believed.

In the meantime, Dr. Jael and Dr. Raclivio, knowing the futility of the experiment and Magor's madness, individually yet collectively worked side by side with him in the laboratory. While he perfected his nanochip, they prepared the babies in the test tubes and the women who would host those babies in their wombs.

Not wanting to be complicit in his madness, the doctors advised Magor of the dangers of his experiment and suggested they experimented on non-life forms first. His response was simply, "Time is running out. Failure is not an option."

Briefly glancing at each other, the doctors nodded in feigned agreement. Although not yet believers in the living God of life, but as believers in the integrity of science and valuing human life, they resolved to thwart his plan at all costs.

# CHAPTER 41

# NANOCHIP

The artificial intelligence transmitted through the nanochip, included the ability to fly like a bird; sustain life underwater like the fish; and it had a code to self-diagnose and self-correct any organ malfunction while decreasing the aging process. It was designed to improve the cellular structure in the body to sustain life in any condition, making them impervious to all internal and external threats, including death.

With the beds filled, phase one of the research was about to commence. Having prepared the women's bodies to receive the developing babies from the test tube, the next step was to transfer them into the womb. Ninety nine percent of the transfers were successful. Within three months, the babies began developing, showing movement and having strong heart beats. They were living beings and many women bonded with the life growing within them.

With the majority of the specimens in their first trimester, the next phase of the experiment was ready to begin. This included inserting the nanochip into each baby's brain, where signals would be sent to improve their development.

Using robotic surgical technology, Magor prepared the nanochip in a syringe, handed it to the doctor, who placed it in the robotic arm to be inserted into the frontal lobe.

Knowing this would be detrimental to the lives of the mothers and babies, and unethical, the doctors pretended to insert the nanochip when in actuality they slipped in into their lab coat pockets and later discarded them in various locations. They then replaced the syringe with innocuous saline fluid that they inserted into the womb while pretending to insert it into the baby's brain. Under the watchful eye of Magor who was glued to the giant monitors as the procedure took place, the doctors, using distraction and sleight of hand techniques, easily fooled him. However, thinking that the nanochip was inserted into the babies' brain, he experimented with different frequencies and signals as he tried to control the brain function. Watching for how the mother and baby were impacted with each change, he grew frustrated, seeing little or no changes. Considering phase one of the experiment a failure, he instructed the doctors to abort all the babies and kill the women so that he could do postmortem forensic examinations to discover why the chips malfunctioned.

Having dedicated her life to saving lives, Dr. Jael was at another crossroads. Crying out to the unseen One whom she believed was the Uncreated Creator of all creation, she desperately needed guidance. The following night, she had a vivid dream where she was in a large open field with beautiful flowers. Each one was distinct in its color, fragrance, texture and design. Looking closer to examine each, she saw the faces of babies peering through the petals. As she was about to pick a flower, an unforgettable voice behind her said, "Do not separate the flower from the stem for I own and created them all." Making the same inquiry to the voice before, she asked, "Who are you?"

This time the voice responded and said, "I AM Yeshua, Jesus Christ, Creator and Savior of all. I have a purpose for everything I create, even the night." Knowing that she was in the presence of majesty, she awoke. Falling to her knees, for the first time in her life, she bowed down and worshipped the true and living God, Yeshua, the Messiah.

CHAPTER 42

# EPIPHANY

With the dream still fresh in her mind, Dr. Jael awoke with a conviction. She had to save the women and babies but was not sure how. Looking up, she said, "I will save the flowers, but you have to show me how."

Suddenly, she had an epiphany that required as much guile and subterfuge as what she had witnessed from the g.l.k himself. Summoning the courage to approach him, she said with much concern, "I have been thinking all night about what may have gone wrong with the experiment. I believe it's because the brain has not developed to the stage where it is capable of neurologically responding to the chip. I am quite sure that your nanochip is perfect, your g.l.k, and the timing of the implant is the problem. Perhaps if we tried again during the second trimester, it will make a difference?"

Turning toward Dr. Raclivio for affirmation, Magor asked, "You're the expert in this department. What are your thoughts?"

Taking his cue from Dr. Jael, Dr. Raclivio responded, "I believe she has a good point. The more developed the brain, the more neurologically functioning it is. The second and third trimesters might be the best time to test this theory. I suggest we wait and see. I'm sure the problem is not with the nanochip, your g.l.k. It's the timing and the babies natural abilities to absorb the frequencies of the chip into their system. Besides, killing the women and aborting the babies now to do forensics will not give us the answers we need."

Contemplating the response, Magor replied, "I see your point. We shall wait and see. In the meantime, I want you both to test for signs of accelerated brain activity."

Seizing the opportunity, Dr. Jael interjected, "It is our pleasure to serve you in whatever capacity you desire in order to make this experiment succeed. However, in order to do so, we will need access to the coding system you have developed. We will do whatever you want."

Automatically looking down and gently stroking his belt buckle, he said, "Let me consider that option. I will let you know tomorrow." He then walked out of the laboratory and exited the building.

Desperate for results, Magor made a decision. The following day, he met with the two doctors and said, "As fellow scientists, I see that you are committed to this experiment and have carefully weighed your proposal." Unconsciously looking down and stroking his belt buckle again, he continued, "It's obvious that I need your expertise to accomplish our goal and will share the coding for the nanochip. I will share the key within a week. In the meantime, I'll expect a daily report of progress as the babies grow in the womb."

Between partially sealed lips, he hissed spewing venom and declared, "If this experiment fails, not only will I kill the women and babies, but you along with them." Not giving them time to respond, he stormed out of the lab, muttering "The GU needs my attention."

# CHAPTER 43

# THE 6$^{TH}$ SEAL

Still furious that his experiment was not going as expected, he summoned his cabinet and demanded an immediate state of the GU report. Ezari Nuka, who assumed the position at his right hand, shared, "Since repairing the malfunction in the Locusts, Snakes and Fish, things are settling into place once again. However, the natives are restless, but the most compliant they have ever been. Fear is good. Being the loyal subjects they are, they have come to depend on you, their g.l.k., for their daily needs. You are their security, provider, hope and joy. While they know you've been focused over the last few months on your research to improve life for them, they still need to see and hear from you. You are their peace."

Hearing what he needed to hear, Magor snarled, "We have created dependent babies. Let's give them what they want. I'll make an address to the GU shortly. But I need something specific to share that will stir up their emotions that compel them to worship me."

Another cabinet member looked to Ezari for permission to speak. Receiving a nod in response, he said, "Your g.l.k., how about sharing your progress with your research and how it will benefit humankind? You're doing the inconceivable and they need to see your creative greatness."

Nodding in approval, Magor responded, "Yes, that is what I need. I will share my progress. Then I want a report of all who did not worship my creative genius. I smell blood and feel the need for another bonfire and soon."

The following day, Magor made his address to the GU:

"My beloved bride, my heart and soul, I know it has been months since my last global communication to all of you. So much has happened and you have been a champion through it all. I want you to know that I have silenced our enemies once again and they have retreated in absolute defeat. Their attack was sudden and unprovoked. But I was ready and counter attacked. Notwithstanding the fact, that we lost a few of our loved ones in the process. Know that I mourn deeply with you. However, in the midst of this trial, it was imperative that I turned my attention to my critical research that will make humankind, you and me, impervious to these hostile and unprovoked attacks."

Pausing for effect, he continued, "At the Nimrod-Romind Research Institute, (NRRI) we have begun this groundbreaking research and I'm delighted to report our immense success. Soon, we will eliminate all limitations and have the ability to fly as the birds, and swim as the fish in the sea. We will self-evolve into a new and more effective human race. With this new creation, I will also delay or eliminate the aging and death process. Fear will be a thing of the past."

With his tone increasing in excitement, he continued, "Within the next few months, we will have our first prototypes on display and we will celebrate as never before. In the meantime, I thank you for your patience as I create a future you can own. One without limits to time, space, air, water or land. You will truly be masters of your own fate. We will be more than conquerors and I will lead you."

The GU exploded in applause as the majority proclaimed his deity and bowed in worship. As they did, the One who held the seven seals in His right hand, opened the sixth seal and, "…Behold, there was a great earthquake; and the sun became black as sackcloth of hair, and the moon became like blood. And the stars of heaven fell to the earth, as a fig tree drops its late figs when it is shaken by a mighty wind. Then the sky receded as a scroll when it is rolled up, and every mountain and island was moved out of its place. And the kings of the earth, the great men, the rich men, the commanders, the mighty men, every slave and every free man, hid themselves in the caves and in the rocks of the mountains, and said to the mountains and rocks, "Fall on us and hide us from the face of Him who sits on the throne and from the wrath of the Lamb! For the great day of His wrath has come, and who is able to stand?" (Revelation 6:12-17)

CHAPTER 44

# THE 7$^{TH}$ SEAL

In an instant, "Everything that could be shaken was shaken, so that the things that could not be shaken may remain." (Hebrews 12:27). All communication satellites were destroyed. The earth's defense weapons, the silver locusts, titanium snakes and steel-like fish, were disarmed and rendered worthless. With the earth quaking beneath their feet and the world steeped in the deepest of darkness, the majority went from worshipping the g.l.k., to screaming, "The end is here, the end is here." People ran helta-skelta in mass pandemonium, trampling each other looking for safety. Finding none, and with fear mounting, hearts exploded while others took their own lives.

The walls of the NRRI fell as an autumn leaf blowing in the wind. Seizing the opportunity to escape, Dr. Jael ran to the birth mothers and said, "Come with me. God of all creation is with us and the babies." Many believed and followed her to safety away from the palace. The rubble from the earthquake created many caves and as if guided by an unseen lighted hand, they moved swiftly and hid in several different caves. In the midst of the devastation, the Remnant who escaped the last persecution, rose up in fearless courage and declared the Word of God to anyone who would listen. Many believed, while others cursed the unseen hand of the enemy they referred to as 'acts of god.'

Hearing the rumble of the earth moving beneath their feet, Magor and his cabinet, shaking and trembling in fear ran to their bunkers. When they arrived, they crouched like newborn babies, crying out and cursing their very existence. Magor shut his eyes, begged for death and commanded his cabinet members to take his life. Still fearing his power and their own lives, they refused to touch him.

When the earth subsided and light emerged, Magor and his cabinet members carefully crawled out from their bunkers. Not knowing what they would find, they laid speechless for some time.

Breaking the silence, they heard the voices as that of a loud multitude crying out, "Salvation belongs to our God who sits on the throne, and to the Lamb!" (Revelation 7:10) As they continued crying out, "All the angels stood around the throne and the elders and the four living creatures, and fell on their faces before the throne and worshiped God, saying,

Amen! Blessing and glory and
wisdom, thanksgiving and honor and power and
might be to our God
forever and ever and ever. Amen."
(Revelation 7:11-12)

Then one of the elders asked, "Who are these arrayed in white robes, and where did they come from?" (Revelation 7:13)

Someone responded, "Sir, you know." (Revelation 7:14)

"So he said to me, 'These are the ones who came out of the great tribulation, and washed their robes and made them white in the blood of the Lamb. Therefore, they are before the throne of God, and serve Him day and night in His temple. And He who sits on the throne will dwell among them. They shall neither hunger anymore nor thirst anymore; the sun shall not strike them, nor any heat; for the Lamb who is in the midst of the throne will shepherd them and lead them to living fountains of waters. And God will wipe away every tear from their eyes.'" (Revelation 7:14-17)

As the earth stood breathlessly still in fear and awe, silence prevailed on the land. The seventh seal was opened, and "there was silence in heaven for about half an hour." (Revelation 8:1) "As it was in heaven, so it was on earth." (Matthew 6:10)

# CHAPTER 45

# UNDERGROUND

Disoriented and shaking with fear, Magor and his cabinet members eventually managed to stand to their feet. Taking in the devastation caused by the earthquake, he declared with feigned confidence, "I shall build again. Not even this can conquer us." Then turning to his cabinet members, he commanded, "Take a body count to see how many survived this attack after you assess the structural damage. In the meantime, I will begin rebuilding our global communication system."

Ezari responded, "Yes, your g.l.k., but it will take some time as we no longer have a universal communication system. We will have to do it manually."

"Don't bother me with details," he barked in frustration. "Take as long as you need. Just get it done as quickly as possible. Send me the strongest males who survived. I need them to begin rebuilding my headquarters immediately. We will need to improvise during this time of rebuilding. We did it before, we will do it again. Let that be the message we spread as you go."

Then looking around, he saw the NRRI laid as a pile of rubble. Assuming that everyone in it was killed, he briefly entertained the idea of relaunching the research. Looking down and stroking his belt buckle, he thought, *We will come back stronger and even more impregnable. This battle may have been won, but the war is far from over. I survived.*

Less than fifty miles from where he stood, a group of over a hundred pregnant women and two doctors, now filled with the Spirit of God, lived concealed in an underground cave. Relying on God for their daily bread and water, they learned to "Live and move and have their being in Him." (Acts 17:28). Over the next six months, the women, ripe with pregnancy began experiencing birth pains. In the course of two weeks, over a hundred babies were born, including multiple twins. Even though they were born in the cave with limited supply of food and water, they were plump and healthy. Most importantly, they did not have the mark of the GU microchip inserted on their arm. Taught by the Spirit, their growth was accelerated and they quickly became living epistles of the gospel of Jesus, Christ, Yeshua.

CHAPTER 46

# UNMASKED

With the electronic mark of the GU disabled, the living epistles were free to move and openly share the gospel of their God, Lord and King. Seizing every opportunity to share the hope found in Christ alone, and no longer under the constant surveillance of the GU, the good news spread even more rapidly in the following decades. In this season, hearts that were previously closed to the truth suddenly opened. Surprisingly, many that were accepting of the truth of the living God, turned from Him in disappointment and disbelief citing that a loving God would not incite such wrath and devastation. Whether opened or closed, all hearts had to decide and own their destiny; either live for God or stand against Him. There was no middle ground.

As an eyewitness to the g.l.k.'s illusion of his stabbing and death, Dr. Jael unmasked his disgraceful mockery of his immortality and resurrection. As her word spread throughout the living epistles (the Remnant) communities, and GU, many citizens believed. Even so, many doubted and remained loyal subjects to their g.l.k.

Now in his sixties, Magor desperately attempted to rise to the same level of dominion, authority and presence he once enjoyed. With his restoration project underway, he began gaining ground. In contrast, the living epistles, including the babies he planned to destroy, grew and multiplied into a formidable force. With a warrior spirit, they challenged the GU's status and contended for truth.

Two living epistles arose from among them. Having been anointed by God, they were granted power to "Prophesy one thousand two hundred and sixty days." (Revelation 11:3) They also had dominion and authority to "Shut heaven, so that no rain fell in the days of their prophecy; and they had power over waters to turn them to blood, and to strike the earth with all plagues, as often as they desired." (Revelation 11:6)

With the GU fragmented and Magor no longer having absolute control, he increased his manipulation and propaganda techniques to incite hatred against the two prophets. Not knowing their names or identities, they were referred to as the two deplorables by the GU. In contrast, they were known as the two witnesses by the Living Epistles. While the Remnant community applauded their tenacity to openly preach the gospel, Magor and his loyal GU followers despised them, and marked them as their primary target to destroy.

On a day like any other, the two witnesses began sharing their testimony when suddenly, a group of GU citizens began chanting, "Long live our king, long live our king." Thinking the crowd was a harmless group who became over excited by the two prophets' testimony, no one was concerned. Until the group began aggressively advancing towards the two prophets, and without time to react, the mob pressed in and trampled them to death. "And their dead bodies lay in the street...then those from the peoples, tribes, tongues, and nations saw their dead bodies for three and a half days and would not allow their dead bodies to be put into graves." (Revelation 11:8-10) However, followers of the g.l.k. rejoiced over their death, had another drunk and disorderly celebration and congratulated each other, because they had overcome the two prophets who tormented them. (Revelation 11:10). Unlike the g.l.k.'s farcical death and resurrection, the breath of life from God entered them after three and a half days of lying dead in the streets. (Revelation 11:11) As they stood on their feet, great fear fell upon those who saw them. And everyone heard a loud voice from heaven called out to them saying, "Come up here." Then the two prophets ascended to heaven in a cloud, and their enemies saw them, including the g.l.k.

"In the same hour, there was another great earthquake, and a tenth of the city fell. In the earthquake seven thousand people were killed and the rest were afraid and gave glory to the God of heaven..." (Revelation 11:12-13) Yet there were many who shook their closed fist towards heaven in greater defiance and inexplicable hatred.

CHAPTER 47

# IMITATION

Never accepting defeat, Magor was determined to discredit the public resurrection and ascension of the two deplorables. Having rebuilt their global communication system, he immediately took to the stage and declared:

"We have been attacked by our enemies in numerous ways over the last few years. These unprovoked attacks threatened our desire for peace, prosperity and security. I know this is your goal as it is mine for you. However, our unseen enemies have opposed us on every front. Now this latest circus, this charade, this ridiculous display of death, resurrection and ascension. My beloved do not believe what you see. Our enemies are crafty and will use every method of illusion to deceive you into believing their false doctrine and power. I will never deceive you. What you thought you saw, was simply a magic trick of smoke and mirrors."

In his most convincing, fatherly tone, he continued, "There was no death. There was no resurrection. There was no ascension. In fact, those two men were imposters masquerading as prophets spreading lies and causing dissension in our peaceful union. No one knew their names or where they came from. They had no credibility. On the other hand, you know me. You know that my brutal stabbing and subsequent death and resurrection were real. Moreover, I'll demonstrate what these mockers attempted to do with their trickery and illusions, then you will believe."

As he finished his sentence, a gunshot was heard, and a large gash appeared on his forehead, immediately spewing blood. He reeled back, squealing in agony. Everyone watching and listening gasped in fear and surprise as they saw his head 'as if it had been mortally wounded.' Then he arose, his deadly wound was healed. And all the world marveled and followed the beast." (Revelation 13:3)

Returning to center stage a few minutes later, as if nothing had occurred, Magor stated in a sarcastic, condescending tone, "Now you see what I mean. Their death, resurrection and ascension were not real, just as I demonstrated. Why believe the false when the truth is before you? I am the truth and deserve your worship."

All blinded to truth believed, even some of the elect Remnant of God.

Persuaded that he won the war, he "Opened his mouth in blasphemy against God, to blaspheme His name, His tabernacle, and those who dwell in heaven." (Revelation 13:6). In a furious rage and with indescribable hatred, Magor strutted with a new level of authority and made war with the saints.

Nonetheless, at the zenith of his pride and arrogance, he was still extremely discontent. The stench of death having become a sweet smelling aroma, especially the death of the deplorables.

Calling his cabinet members to him, he asked the familiar question, "What's next?"

Ezari Nuka, advised, "I've seen life-sized images of you in my dreams and all people were bowing down in continual worship."

Elated with the prospect of continuous worship, Magor decided to make life-sized images of himself and strategically placed them throughout the GU. Without commanding worship, many bowed before the statues, pledging their allegiance to the idols. With no regard for God nor humanity, he continued waging war against the unseen enemy and the deplorables, leaving a trail of death wherever he desired.

With the mystery of lawlessness now overflowing, war was declared, "Won," before it began.

## CHAPTER 48

# NOW WHAT? AGAIN & AGAIN

With unleashed hatred and boundless authority, over time, Magor fortified the GU stronger than before. The AI, (artificial intelligent), robotic locusts, snakes and fish were improved and a new sense of security returned to the globe. Bored with the periodic scrimmages to eliminate the deplorables, he turned his attention to securing his legacy. Even though he believed in his immortality, he thought that he needed at least two sons to carry on his name.

Following in his father's footsteps, he initiated the tubular conception and began searching for a doctor whom he could trust with the process. Knowing that Dr. Jael and Dr. Raclivio were the best doctors in their field, he initiated a search for either one. Even though he believed they might have been killed in the devasting earthquake a few years prior with the collapse of the NRRI, he wanted confirmation. He, therefore, commanded his cabinet to find out if they were alive.

After issuing a search and find bulletin across the GU, Dr. Jael's name finally appeared on a long list of suspected deplorables. Eager to share with the g.l.k., Ezari Nuka reported, "We found one of the doctors on your list, my g.l.k. Unfortunately, she is listed as a potential deplorable. It appears that someone who was once a deplorable but is now one of your devoted subjects reported her name to us."

Responding with disbelief, Magor said, "I find that hard to believe. Dr. Jael was one of my four brides and one of two doctors with whom I worked side by side for months on my experiment. Surely there would have been some indication of her disloyalty to me then. Didn't you also thoroughly examine her to ensure that she was a loyal GU citizen to have selected her as one of the final four brides? There must be some mistake. I find it hard to believe. Bring her in, I need to know for myself."

The following week, a much older image of Dr. Jael stood before Magor. Looking at her quizzically he said, "It has been some time since we lost contact with you. I assumed you died along with everyone else when the NRRI collapsed. What happened? Where have you been? And why is your name on our list of enemies of the GU?"

Led by the spirit of God, she bowed her head in feigned respect, and replied, "I miraculously survived the earthquake, your g.l.k. Without going into the long story of the past, after the earthquake, there was so much devastation that I dedicated my time and expertise to helping those who needed medical care, and there were many as you already know. There was much work to do, and not enough doctors to help. As to how my name got on the list of deplorables, I don't know. I am a loyal citizen. My commitment is to serve and to heal."

"But as one of my four regional brides, why didn't you at least let me know that you were still alive?" Magor asked.

Dr. Jael replied, still with her head bowed, "I am but a humble servant and didn't even think you noticed my presence or absence."

Hearing what he wanted to hear and impressed by her humility, Magor replied, "I forgive you. Now I need your expert medical assistance as I've decided to have children. Preferably two sons and perhaps one daughter and I need someone whom I can trust with the entire process. I don't want to randomly select the birth mothers. I need to know they are biologically and mentally fit for the task. I will personally oversee the mental aspect but need your expertise to confirm their biological readiness to successfully carry my children to full term."

Prompted by the spirit, she replied, "Yes, your g.l.k. I would also need to give you a thorough physical. When would you like to begin?"

Eager to get the process started, Magor replied, "Let's begin tomorrow. However, I don't see the need for my physical. I'm immortal, remember and therefore in perfect condition. I've had my seeds frozen some time ago. It's stored and waiting to fertilize. Nonetheless, if that's what the doctor needs to guarantee a successful outcome, so be it. You can conduct my physical in my private quarters as I don't want the eyes of the GU watching."

Seeing an opportunity before her, she replied, "It would be an honor to serve my King," She then asked, "How else may I serve you?"

Satisfied with her submissiveness, he stated, "I'll see you tomorrow."

CHAPTER 49

# HISTORY REPEATED

The following day, Dr. Jael arrived with her medical equipment to facilitate Magor's physical. Being a keen observer of her environment, she noticed everything about his private quarters. Once inside, she noticed that he was wearing a robe having removed his shirt. However, he was still wearing his pants and belt with the unique large silver clasp.

Without waiting for a greeting, he said, "I have a very busy day ahead of me. Let's get this over with as quickly as possible. I've already removed my shirt for the examination. I always keep my pants and belt close to me at all times, so you will need to work around them." Then he asked suspiciously, "Exactly what are you going to do?"

She meekly replied, "I will take all fluid samples and then examine you physically. I can complete the examination just as you are. If that is okay with you?"

Then guiding him to one of his sofas, she reached into her medical bag and pulled out a syringe as she prepared to first take blood samples. When she found a viable vein, she swiftly switched the syringe and injected his arm with a large dose of fentanyl. His body immediately went limp in unconsciousness. Then continuing to act quickly, she pulled out a long, thin scalpel and skillfully pierced it through his heart. *Now let's see how immortal you truly are?* she thought to herself, as his breath and blood seeped from his body.

She then reached for his belt with the large silver buckle that he frequently caressed. Convinced that it was more than a belt buckle, she tried opening it, but to no avail. It then dawned on her to use his right hand and gently push in its sides. To her amazement, the silver flap of the buckle flipped open revealing a set of small lights flashing at different intervals. Confirming her suspicions, she knew this was the remote control master key to unlock his inventions.

Not knowing what to do next, she gingerly removed the belt. Then reaching for a miniature statue of himself, (which was the prototype of the life-sized statues), she smashed the buckle as fine as she could. As she did, the sound as that of thunder, and metal crashing was released. The earth began quaking as the silver locusts, titanium snakes and steel-like fish malfunctioned and then stopped as if dead. Their malfunctioning triggered a subsequent chain reaction on the earth, the ocean and the sky. Hot sparks of scorching lava spewed from the ground covering its surface in various places. Earthquakes of immeasurable magnitudes violently erupted causing even mountains to implode. The oceans bulged forming tidal waves with intense gravitational force that raced towards the earth. As the silver locusts discombobulated in the sky, it appeared as if the stars were falling like red, fiery blood.

Feeling as if the walls were caving in, Dr. Jael looked for an exit. Finding none, she peacefully sat and prayed. Within minutes, the walls crashed in around her, smashing Magor Romind's body to powder, but it did not come near her. It, however, exposed a set of stairs leading out of the room. As if guided by an unseen hand, she moved down the stairs, then through a winding passage that led out to a luxurious bunker filled with food and water. Exhausted by the adrenaline coursing through her body, she looked up and said, "I've finished the work," then laid down and fell peacefully to sleep.

It was the worst devastation the earth had ever experienced. Yet as quickly as it began, it ended, and stillness covered the earth.

# CHAPTER 50

# PRETENSE

Believing she was dreaming, Dr. Jael heard footsteps and voices shouting, "Our g.l.k., are you in there? Are you okay?"

Her heart began racing as she regained consciousness from her deep sleep. Knowing the penalty would be public execution for what she had done, she looked up and said to herself, "I'm ready to live or die for you, my Lord. My life is and always has been in your hands."

Minutes later, about ten GU Inspectors, followed by Ezari Nuka and other cabinet members, rushed towards her and asked, "Where's the g.l.k?"

Still groggy from her deep sleep, she replied weakly, "I don't know. I was doing his physical when suddenly the earth began shaking and the walls caved in. Then I saw the entrance to stairs and began running towards the opening. Isn't the g.l.k. here? Did he escape?"

Barking an order to the GU Inspectors, Ezari yelled, "Search beneath every rock and brick until you find him. If he isn't here, then we can assume that he did not escape as there is only dust and rubble that the eye can see." Then looking at her suspiciously, he remarked, "It's a miracle that you escaped."

Responding in a weak voice, she replied, "It is a miracle. I truly thought I was going to die. What happened?" She asked innocently.

"We're trying to figure that out." Ezari answered, then asked "What was the last thing you remember?"

"I was doing the g.l.k's physical as he requested. He was lying on the sofa. Then the sudden earthquake, sounds of thunder and the ceiling and walls began crashing in. Then I saw this staircase and ran for my life. Unfortunately, I don't know what the g.l.k did?"

As she finished speaking, an inspector came and said, "There are no signs of the g.l.k, other than his clothes covered in dust. It appears that he may have been crushed to powder. We will bring in a forensics team to confirm."

Taking command, Ezari instructed the GU Inspectors and the other cabinet members, "Let's keep this to ourselves for now until it is confirmed. This was the most devasting disaster by far and we need time to communicate our recovery plan. As the second in command, I will assume leadership until we confirm the death of our beloved g.l.k. In the meantime, let's assess the overall damage within the GU and begin drafting a recovery plan. Report back to me tomorrow." Then looking at Dr. Jael, he continued, "As for you, we will keep you in custody until we confirm your story."

The following week she was released, having served her purpose.

CHAPTER 51

# THE CABINET

Seizing the opportunity to solidify his command as the next GU leader, Ezari called the cabinet together for an emergency meeting. Wasting no time, he stated, "As the second in command, I am taking immediate leadership of the GU. Does anyone have objections?"

One cabinet member arrogantly replied, "We don't dispute that you're the second in command under Magor's leadership, but he is dead. There is no way he could have survived if he was in that room when the earthquake hit. I believe he is finally dead this time. This is a new beginning. I believe we need to vote on it."

"Are you challenging my authority?" Ezari asked threateningly.

Another cabinet member said, "What authority? The only authority you had was while Magor was alive. He was the one with authority, you were one of us until Zukorain Sedski disappeared."

Other cabinet members, vying for position joined in and echoed the same sentiment. Angry and frustrated, Ezari snarled, "This is treasonous. How dare you question my authority?"

A cabinet member angrily yelled, "How dare you assume that you're the next leader of the GU? Remember, before the nations became one global unit, we were all leaders in our own right, among our people, with our own identity, language, authority and power. We united because Magor held the master key that could destroy the world if he wanted to. What do you hold? I say we vote on who we want to lead us, or even if we want one person to lead the entire GU. Everything is up for grabs, and I personally intend to take back what belonged to me and my forefather's nation."

Knowing that he was outnumbered and wanting to buy time, Ezari said, "I'm willing to listen. Perhaps this is an opportunity for a new beginning. What do you propose?"

"I propose that we dismantle the union and re-draw the lines of the nations as they were before Magor commandeered control. That each of us take our rightful position as leaders of our forefather's land and allow the citizens to choose where they want to live. We can continue as a global union but consisting of many nations and leaders with equal authority."

Trying to hide his frustration, Ezari inquired, "And how do you propose we dismantle all that we've worked to achieve over the last few decades? Most importantly, how do you propose to get the GU citizens to embrace these changes? Perhaps we need to pause and rethink our next steps carefully. After all, Magor may be alive and we're all still reeling from the recent devastation ourselves. Let's re-assemble next week. In the meantime, I will act as the interim leader. Can we all agree with this strategy?"

Looking at each other with suspicion, they nodded in agreement. Immediately following the meeting, Ezari issued an order to the GU Inspectors to seize the twenty-three cabinet members and publicly hang them as traitors.

While their bodies were stiffening with the disfigurement of death, Ezari took center stage having enabled the emergency broadcasting system, and made his first public announcement:

"As you all know by now, our beloved g.l.k., Magor G. Romind, is now resting with his forefathers in death. We will have a memorial the world has never seen to honor this great man who served, protected and provided for us all his life. We will celebrate, worship and praise him even more in death than in life. While the circumstances of his death are still unclear, we know that there were diabolic, evil traitors within his own cabinet. Self-serving, self-seeking, narcissist, power hungry men and women who constantly plotted to disrupt the unity of our neatly ordered world (N.O.W). I have finally eliminated this threat and will serve you, with the same fervor as our beloved g.l.k. We will rebuild and become an even stronger force than before. This is my promise to you.

Let me assure you, that knowing his time was short, our g.l.k., made plans for our future. His final instruction to me, as his second in command, was to raise his children. Yes, I said his children. Even facing death, he was thinking of you.

In preparation for his departure, he made provision for his seed to bring new life. And we will begin that process as soon as the dust is settled. Within the next year, his children will be born. Unable to seed children myself, the g.l.k. had asked me to raise his own, should he be unable to do so. It is my honor and duty to serve you, him, and his children. His children, our children are our posterity. With his DNA, (Deoxyribonucleic Acid), coursing through their veins, in time they will lead us to unparalleled greatness. Rest assured that our g.l.k. will live on through his offspring." With his tone rising a few octaves, he ended by declaring, "This is not an ending, but a new beginning."

## CHAPTER 52

# NOW – OWN - WON

Now, the earth experienced many more seasons of devastating plagues with intermittent seasons of peace. Following in Magor Romind's footsteps, Ezari Nuka temporarily assumed leadership of the GU, but without much success.

Ultimately, the Global Union was once again divided into separate nations, languages, tongues and tribes. The Living Epistles, bearing the mark of God in their heart, and on their forehead, continually faced persecution for their faith in the Living God. Those committed to darkness remained blinded by their darkness, refusing to acknowledge the light. They eagerly followed any leader who identified with them in their darkness, proudly surrendering their bodies as marquees of their allegiance.

Magor Romind's seeds were successfully fertilized and implanted in wombs that produced life. With his DNA, and that of his forefather's, his offspring owned their destinies. Each one, male and female, rising to leadership in their own right, battled against each other and against the living epistles whose names were written in the Book Of Life.

Many battles were fought, but the war was won by the one and only true and living God, King of kings and Lord of Lords, and those who followed Him to the end. They are the ones who dwelt in "...the Holy City, New Jerusalem coming down out of heaven from God, prepared as a bride adorned for her husband...Behold, the tabernacle of God is with men, and He will dwell with them, and they shall be His people. God Himself shall be with them and be their God. And God will wipe away every tear from their eyes; there will be no more death, nor sorrow, nor crying. There shall be no more pain, for the former things have passed away."

Then He who sat on the throne said, "Behold, I make all things new...For these words are true and faithful...It is done! I am the Alpha and the Omega, the Beginning and the End. I will give of the fountain of water of life freely to him who thirsts. He who overcomes shall inherit all things, and I will be his God and he shall be My son. But the cowardly, unbelieving, abominable, murderers, sexually immoral, sorcerers, idolaters, and all liars shall have their part in the lake which burns with fire and brimstone, which is the second death." (Revelation 21:2-8)

"...And behold, I am coming quickly, and My reward is with me, to give to everyone according to his work. I am the Alpha and the Omega, the Beginning and the End, the First and the Last. Blessed are those who do His commandments, that they may have the right to the tree of life and may enter through the gates into the city." (Revelation 22:12-13)

# CHAPTER 53

# WON

It was over. The war was won. The battles for dominion, authority and presence that began in the heavenlies, were finished. The mystery of lawlessness conceived when Lucifer and one third of the angels fell from heaven, was done. Heaven and earth were now fully populated with God's Living Epistles and a new earth emerged. A new timeless age was beginning. Paradise. The Garden of Eden once again pulsated with eternal life as the curse of death, hell and the grave were forever swallowed up in His victory.

Yeshua, Adonai Tzva'ot, God of Heaven's Armies, returned victorious, just as He said. Striding as a ferocious lion, King of Heaven and Earth, He chained His adversaries, locked the impenetrable prison doors and threw away the keys. It was now and forever sealed.

"The devil, who deceived them (the saints) was cast into the lake of fire and brimstone where the beast and the false prophet are. And they will be tormented day and night forever and ever." (Revelation 20:10)

Then it happened. Suddenly. Unexpectantly. On a day unlike any other. A great mystery was revealed "…We shall not all

179

sleep (die), but we shall all be changed - in a moment, in the twinkling of an eye, at the last shofar. For the shofar will sound, and the dead will be raised incorruptible, and we shall be changed. For this corruptible (body) must put on incorruption, and this mortal (body) must put on immortality." (1 Corinthians 15:5-53)

With His garments soaked with the blood of His enemies, our conquering King, Yeshua, took His seat on the "Great white throne of judgement." (Revelation 20:11) And then "...Books were opened. And another book was opened, which is the Book of Life. And the dead were judged according to their works, by the things which were written in the books. The sea gave up the dead who were in it, and Death and Hades delivered up the dead who were in them. And they were judged, each one according to his works. Then Death and Hades were cast into the lake of fire. This is the second death. And anyone not found written in the Book of Life was cast into the lake of fire." (Revelation 20:12-15)

As it was in heaven, so it was on earth. (Matthew 6:10) The Father answered the Son's prayer, that "They may be one, as We are one. Just as You, Father, are united with Me and I with You. I pray that they may be united with Us...The glory which You have given to me, I have given to them; so that they may be one, just as We are one. I united with them and You with Me, so that they may be completely one..." (John 17:20-23)

With His limitless power, this conquering King had the ability to speak the Word and the earth, having been depleted by the former reign of darkness, could have been completely restored to its former glory. But always choosing partnership and relationship, He invited and welcomed His chosen to reign with Him, as kings and priests, on earth as it is in heaven. (Revelation 5:10) It was the beginning of a final new and unending exhilarating era.

CHAPTER 54

# TRANSFORMATION

From the four corners of the world, bodies miraculously joined with spirit. Wheat separated from chaff; bone from marrow; and sheep from goats. Those ascended chose to eat from the tree of life (Yeshua). Their names were written in the Lamb's Book of Life and they bore the name of their King on their forehead. (Revelation 22:4) While those choosing to eat of the tree of the knowledge of good and evil, descended into the abyss. Each receiving the consequences of their choices while on earth. Those who descended, cursed God and lived horrifically in continuous dying and death, in an eternal fire. While those ascended praised God and lived; never to taste death.

In the blink of the eye, the earth that once moaned and groaned from the weight of sin, death and destruction, was rescued. There was no night, nor darkness as the Son's presence illuminated heaven and earth. (Revelation 22:5) The trees, therefore, perked up in anticipation of new life and light. Sprouting colors never before seen on the earth they swayed to the pure sound of heaven's frequencies. Flowers emerged in glorious array. Caressed by gentle winds, they dispersed their scintillating fragrance continuously glorifying their Creator. Soothing sounds as that of a myriad of waterfalls entertained the ear, and creatures of every kind, frolicked in jubilant delight. At last, heaven and earth danced as one.

As the caterpillar emerging as a butterfly, transformation broke through. When body and spirit reunited, a new being was formed. Spirit took on flesh and prepared to reign, rule and dominate the earth in relationship with its Creator. (Genesis 2:15) As it was in the beginning, so it was again.

Unlike the butterfly however, those transformed into their glorified bodies, remembered their former likeness. Observing the newness around them, including their skin that glowed as if sprinkled with fine gold dust; unveiled eyes that could see all things; a keen sense of hearing, even the lowest of whispers; trees clapping their hands as they swayed to the gentle breeze; flowers softly humming to a new frequency; sensitivity to touch that tingled and sent wave upon wave of exhilarated delight, the smell of fresh fragrances never before experienced; the revealed sons (and daughters) of God spent as much time as needed becoming acquainted with their new resurrected bodies, new abilities, authority, and dominion.

In this eternal, timeless realm now called heaven on earth, the beginning of change was ignited. A new world order was emerging. While the King of kings could speak the word, and all things would be perfected, He chose to engage His kings and priests in the change initiative.

Guided by the Holy Spirit, each found their new home. It was a place uniquely prepared for them, complete with more than they could think of or imagine. (John 14:3) & (Ephesians 3:20:21) In awe of their new surroundings, all bowed in worship and thanksgiving. Overcome with its beauty and a Presence they instinctively knew to be that of their beloved King, they continuously praised Yeshua. Allowing time to explore, get re-acquainted with loved ones and meet new friends, they temporarily rested in the joy of knowing they were finally home.

# CHAPTER 55

# DELIGHT

With the government on His shoulder, (Isaiah 9:6) the Son of God, Son of Man declared with exuberant joy and indescribable delight: "Father, it is truly finished. We are finally one. (John 17) Everyone We have chosen and who has chosen Us, are with Us where We are. (John 14:3). Your will is done on earth as it is in heaven. (Matthew 6:10) I'm ready to receive my reward, my Bride, and together we shall rebuild and restore our Kingdom on earth to its former glory as it is heaven."

"I am so proud of You my Son. You accomplished all, and more, that I desired You to do. I have a surprise reward for You that I have been saving "for such a time as this." (Esther 4:14). One that is my delight to do. It's Your public coronation. You are, always has and always will be King of kings and Lord of lords. Everyone knows this. Nonetheless, I want to publicly present You, my Beloved Son, again, and again to the world. We have the ages to come to rebuild, restore and renew. Let's begin with Your public coronation and royal wedding. There is much to celebrate."

Humbled by this unexpected reward, the Son bowed to the Father and said, "You are truly a good Father. Do as You desire, for Your Will is My desire. I have this one request, that everyone in the kingdom participates in the planning, for it's not only my public crowning but theirs as well."

"Son, your wish is my delight and desire also. It is done. Now let's get busy with the planning. Let me know when it's ready. I'm eager to crown You, and for Us to distribute crowns on that day. This will be the first of many celebrations in Our New World."

# CHAPTER 56

# HEADQUARTERS

With the Son of Man's birthplace and ancestors of Jewish descent, He set up His world headquarters in Jerusalem. As described by one of His disciples, the Apostle John, who saw in the spirit "...the great city, the holy Jerusalem, descending out of heaven from God, having the glory of God. Her light was like a most precious stone, like a jasper stone, clear as crystal. Also, she had a great and high wall with twelve gates, and twelve angels at the gates, and the names written on them, which are the names of the twelve tribes of the children of Israel: three gates on the east, three gates on the north, three gates on the south, and three gates on the west.

Now the wall of the city had twelve foundations, and there were the names of the twelve apostles of the Lamb...The city is laid out as a square; its length is as great as its breadth....Its length, breadth, and height are equal...The construction of its wall was of jasper; and the city was pure gold, like clear glass.

The foundations of the wall of the city were adorned with all kinds of precious stones: the first foundation was jasper, the second sapphire, the third chalcedony, the fourth emerald, the fifth sardonyx, the sixth sardius, the seventh chrysolite, the eight beryl, the ninth topaz, the tenth chrysoprase, the eleventh jacinth, and the twelfth amethyst.

The twelve gates were twelve pearls; each individual gate was of one pearl. And the street of the city was pure gold, like transparent glass.

The city had no need of the sun or of the moon to shine in it, for the glory of God illuminated it. The Lamb is its light. And the nations of those who are saved shall walk in its light, and the kings of the earth bring their glory and honor into it. Its gates shall not be shut at all by day (there shall be no night there)." (Revelation 21:10-26)

Even though the Kings presence was felt throughout the nations, His headquarters was the epicenter of all international and national affairs. It was where He set up the seat of His government. The place from which all things, including spiritual, economic, social, agricultural, political, administrative, educational and judicial, etc., flowed. It was the pulse and heart of heaven and earth.

CHAPTER 57

# INFRASTRUCTURE

Honored by His Father's desire, the Son called the twenty-four elders to the throne room at the Headquarters. These were His faithful and true worshippers, "Clothed in white garments, and (wore) golden crowns on their heads. And from the throne proceeded lightnings, thunderings, and voices..." Saying:

"Holy, Holy, Holy,
Lord God Almighty
Who was and is and is to come!"
(Revelations 4:4-5)

As the twenty-four elders approached the throne they joined in the continuous worship and would fall down before Him who sits on the throne and worship Him who lives forever and ever, and cast their crowns before the throne saying:

"You are worthy, O Lord,
To receive glory and honor and power;
For You created all things,
And by Your will they exist and were created."

When the elders took their seat around the throne, the Son greeted them and said, "It is always my pleasure seeing you all."

The elders automatically bowed before Him and waited in silence for His next words. The Son continued, "We have accomplished much. We have witnessed the battles. We have prayed and interceded together. We have cried over the loss of loved ones who chose not to have their names written in the book of life. Unfortunately, they are receiving the reward of their choices. Nevertheless, we did all we could for them and in tears gave them over to their will. Now the battles are over. The war is won. It is finished. We have much planning and work ahead. But first, the Father wants to commemorate the beginning of our new world with a coronation and wedding ceremony. A ceremony in which everyone is engaged. Our first unified event as one people, in heaven and on earth. Knowing the Father, He has many other surprises ahead. I have an idea of some, but He even surprises Me at times. I know He will provide golden crowns to all who chose to eat of the tree of life. To all who chose the Kingdom of Heaven as their citizenship while on earth and Me as their Sovereign King. But we need to have a master plan on how to engage everyone according to their talents and interests. Where do we begin?"

Excited by the question the twenty-four elders bowed before the Son and waited in silence for the Holy Spirit to fill their hearts with ideas and strategies. Intuitively knowing the thoughts of the spirit within them, one elder shared, "We need to begin at the beginning and create an infrastructure within each nation, tribe, and tongue."

Another shared, "This means we will need to create governmental systems and structures."

Yet another shared, "We will need to know everyone's talents and interests."

Another added, "We need to implement a similar structure as Moses did leading the children of Israel in the desert. Just as he formed a nation out of a band of slaves, we will form nations. We need to identify heads of Nations, heads of state, heads of cities, tribes and towns."

Excited with the direction of the discussion, another chimed in and shared, "Yes, we need to break it down to the lowest level of leaders. Then we can engage them in identifying those with qualifications to plan and execute this extraordinary global event."

"These are critical appointments. What criteria will we use to make our selections?" another inquired.

Seizing the opportunity, the Son replied, "The criteria is simple. We select those whose hearts are fully surrendered to Me. Who, having never seen Me, loved and obeyed Me to the end. (John 20:29) Those who walked by the spirit and did not fulfill the lust of the flesh. (Galatians 5:16-17) Especially those who gave their lives for My sake. They are the ones prepared for Kingdom leadership who stored up treasure in heaven." (Matthew 6:19-20)

"I believe this will come as a surprise to many who stored up treasure on earth. Who led large ministries but whose hearts were not devoted to You," another elder remarked with much sadness.

"Whatever the outcome, all will know that our decisions are just and true," another elder added.

"Well said," remarked the Son with a smile in His voice. "Let's begin the selection process."

CHAPTER 58

# DISTINCTION

With the criteria clearly outlined, and the Book of Life available at their fingertips, the Son of Man and the twenty-four elders began the selection process. Beginning with identifying forty-eight kings for each of the nations, they narrowed down the list to the final hundred.

This list included an unsuspected minority of martyrs, those who boldly lived and died for Christ. Those whose heart belonged to Him, who obeyed in the small as well as the big things. Those like Job, who decided that even though He may slay them, they trusted in Him. (Job 13:15) Many who lived in the shadows, storing up treasure in heaven, counting their lives as nothing, so that God would be all. (Acts 20:24)

They were the ones often unnoticed, who loved and gave thanks without ceasing nor complaining. (1 Thessalonians 5:18) The ones who suffered silently without complaint or murmuring, praising, worshipping and patiently waiting, believing and depending on God. The ones determined not to have any confidence in their flesh, and daily picked up their crosses, followed Him through the darkness and storms of their earthly life. (Luke 9:23) They ate of the tree of life and counted their life as loss to gain the knowledge of God. (Philippians 3:8)

They were the ones who were hated by the world yet applauded by heaven. They presented their bodies as a living sacrifice, holy and acceptable to God as their reasonable service of worship with joy and delight. (Romans 12:1) Loving God first with all their heart, mind, and soul, they loved their neighbor as themselves, (Matthew 22:36-40) They were the redeemed of the Lord who humbly bore the image of their God, Lord and King. (2 Corinthians 3:18)

Surprising to many, but not surprising to the Son, the list included many unborn leaders. Those who were aborted while in the womb, never receiving the opportunity to fulfill their destiny on the earth. Their record remained unblemished as a testimony of their faith. And the Son, sovereignly knowing all things, knew their end from the beginning. These were the ones discarded without worth on earth but counted as worthy in heaven. Their heavenly names were stamped and recorded and they were on the list of high potentials for Kingdom leadership.

After a healthy exchange of thoughts and ideas, the list was narrowed down to eighty. Continuing to separate bone from marrow, they narrowed it down to fifty and continued splitting hairs until they identified the final forty-eight.

As they were completing the list, one elder shared a divine epiphany, "Let's make this a rotational position, so that others have the opportunity to serve in this important role and no one feels stuck or bored serving in this capacity or any other capacity for eternity."

"You've read my mind, my friend," the Son of Man remarked. "And we are assuming that they will accept this role. Remember, they will have the will to choose this assignment when offered to them. Be prepared, some may decline, preferring to do something else as everything is voluntary in our Kingdom. We cannot enforce our will upon anyone. We desire voluntary service, out of a heart of love as there's no place for religion, nor the religious." Pausing with a big grin on His face, He further added, "But this I'm sure of with this group, if they unwaveringly chose the Father's will while on earth, they will even more joyfully choose His will now. So, whatever their decision, it's a win/win for all."

Excited to share their strategy with the forty-eight potential heads of nations, the Son and the Elders drafted an invitation.

CHAPTER 59

# INVITATION

In the timelessness of eternity, in what appeared to be an instant, the forty-eight identified potential leaders of nations, received a sealed envelope. Not knowing how or when the invitation was delivered, each noticed the beautiful red, raised legal seal with the letter "A" stamped in the center. Outlined on the embossed, gold trimmed envelope, the return address simply stated,

"From the office of your King and Friend,
World Headquarters,
Jerusalem"

Without knowing what it contained, each gently kissed the envelope and touched it with tenderness that brought happy tears to their eyes. Anticipating their first official meeting with their King and friend, their heart accelerated with unleashed excitement and expectation. The moment they had been waiting for all their lives was about to unfold, meeting their King, face to face, in a private setting for the first time.

Glinda Rhoot, (ref. R7:17 Trilogy: Dominion, Authority and Presence - Beyond Limits) was among the forty-eight who received an invitation. Her face, glowing with delight without opening the envelope, fell to her knees and responded as she always did, and said, "Yes." The others responded in like manner. All said "Yes," before knowing the contents of the envelope and worshipped. Finally rising from their knees, each kissed the seal and the envelope before opening it.

Each invitation was personalized with the name of the recipient and was handwritten:

Glinda,

How I have longed for this moment when we meet face to face. We have loved you and chose you before the foundation of this world (Ephesians 1:4) Please join me and our twenty-four elders, who have prayed for you and have loved you. You are one of our precious champions on earth, and we look forward to partnering with you in our new world. An angel will accompany you to us. Holy Spirit has and as always, will prepare you.

Your Beloved King and Friend,
Son of God, Son of Man
Adonai, Yeshua, Jesus Christ, the Messiah

## CHAPTER 60

# FIRSTS

When Glinda and the other forty-seven priests and kings (Revelation 1:6) read the invitation, their hearts soared with anticipation. Knowing where they were going, but not knowing how they would get there from where they were located around the world, they waited with anticipation for their angelic hosts.

Then it happened. A familiar voice called their name and said, "Come up here." Looking up, they saw two beings, covered in white linen, with their hands outstretched. Reaching to take their hand, they saw large wings, as that of an eagle protruding from their upper back. With the face of a human, eyes in front and behind, legs and mane of a lion and the agility of a cheetah, they greeted their human charge with a friendly, welcoming smile.

Overwhelmed with the newness of it all, each returned the greeting. Then the angelic beings gently hoisted them on their broad horse-like back and instructed them to hold on to their mane. Speaking if only spoken to, the angelic beings remained silent, waiting for their charge to speak. After what appeared to be a few minutes,

Glinda relaxed and began enjoying the ride and the scenery.

"This is the most exciting thing I've ever done," she remarked breathlessly. "What is your name?"

Excited to know his charge, the angelic being replied, "Our name is Speed and we can transport you anywhere you like. Of course, you can go wherever you like as well, but that's a lesson you will learn over time. Today we are going to the world Headquarters."

No sooner had they begun a conversation, than they arrived at the destination. In fact, all forty-eight invitees arrived simultaneously in the courtyard of the world capital. Looking around in awe and wonder, they marveled at the pearl gates, the golden, jewel-lined foundation they stood on, the intricate architecture but most importantly, the unique beings, each exceptionally designed, who freely walked around leaving a trail of joy, laughter and excitement in the atmosphere. In the background they heard the gentle hum of voices lifted in worship all expressing the same melody:

"You are worthy, O Lord,
To receive glory and honor and power;
For You created all things,
And by Your will they exist and were created."

Mesmerized by the sound, they looked in the direction from where it was emanating. Thinking they would see a heavenly choir, they were amazed to see water cascading in a gentle fall flowing over colorful rocks from the foundation, through the courtyard, and out from the magnificent city. As the water flowed, they released songs of worship and each one heard the lyrics in his/her own language. Resisting the temptation to bow in worship, they stood still, speechless and waited.

CHAPTER 61

# FIRST SIGHT

The King, just as eager to meet and greet His friends, walked through the exquisite golden doors. Dressed simply in a long-sleeved shirt and pants with a plain, casual jacket, He moved slowly yet purposefully. His dark, wavy hair looked somewhat disheveled. The Son of Man looked like a young image of His ancestor, King David. Mistaking Him for the gardener, the forty-eight guests saw Him but didn't pay much attention as He approached them. Then reaching out His nail scarred hand to greet them, they realized who He was and fell dumb-struck at His feet.

After some time, they rose to their knees with a brilliant light, as that of the sun reflecting from their eyes as they gazed upon the One they loved. Glinda gently stroked His nail scarred hand and echoed what everyone else was thinking, "I've imagined this unimaginable day, and it is so much more than I could ever have thought or imagined. I am actually here, touching the scars that You bore for me. How do I say thanks? How my King, may I serve you?"

Laughing with delight, He bent down to lift each one to their feet. As He did, His perfectly white teeth contrasted against His smooth olive, sun tanned skin. Then greeting each one by name and hugging them individually and then in a group hug, He said, "I have been waiting for this day more than you could ever imagine. You and Our Father are the joy that was set before Me that enabled me to endure the cross. (Hebrews 12:2) I would do it all over again. Let's get inside. We've got much to catch up on and discuss."

Still speechless and in awe of His unassuming yet powerful presence, the forty-eight followed Him as sheep with their Shepherd. Walking through a marble hallway, they entered a large open space that was lined with exotic flowering plants, some they recognized but many they didn't. The marble floor shimmered with colorful lights that radiated with each step He took. Softly flowing waterfalls hummed melodious praise, thanksgiving and worship at the sound of His coming. All manner of uniquely designed creatures, with eyes surrounding their bodies moved in perfect synchronization, yet were always focused on the One who sat on a very unusual throne.

It was the only furnishing that was made of natural, unpolished wood. There was no incredible design, just plain wood. Upon closer examination, flecks of red, as that of blood soaked into the porous substance, was visible. With their eyes riveted on that simple, yet exquisite seat, the invitees instinctively knew it was His throne that was made from the cross on which He died for their sins.

There were twenty four other thrones in the room. Twelve on each side of the wooden throne creating an open, oval formation. Each one was made of purest gold inlaid with all manner of precious stones that glistened with all hues of the rainbow. Names of the twenty elders were carved in the backs of each chair in silver outlined with rubies. In the middle of the oval, there was a low table with comfortable red cushions with the name of each invitee inscribed in gold. The table was filled with colorful drinks and a variety of fruits and vegetables appealing to the eye, touch, smell, and taste.

Captivated by the majesty of their surroundings, the forty-eight gazed in awe as their eyes rested on the thrones and the names of the ones who sat on them. Some they recognized, others they didn't. Among them were Abraham, Isaac, Jacob (Israel), Joseph, Moses, Samuel, King David, Elijah, Daniel, Esther, Peter, James, John, Paul, other kings, priests and prophets and Mary, the mother of the Son of Man, and His earthly father, Joseph.

Although impressed with the names of the twenty-four elders, their eyes were fixed on the one blood soaked wooden throne. As the Son of Man, Yeshua, took His seat, the twenty-four elders suddenly appeared. When they entered they chanted along with the water symphony in praise and adoration. With each step they removed their spectacular golden crowns and laid it at His feet. Joining in the worship, the invitees bowed low in awe and reverence before their King.

CHAPTER 62

# HONOR

In the timelessness of eternity, the elders and the invitees praised and worshipped the Son of Man. Then He rose from His seat of honor and all stood silently before Him. Breaking the silence He said, "Thank you. There's lots to discuss and decisions to be made. What we decide now, will be foundational to everything we're building. I know introductions are usually made at the beginning, but for this meeting, I'd like to delay it until the end." Then laughing to Himself, He remarked, "You know we like to do the unexpected, and there's purpose in everything we do. Let's say I'm saving the best for last. Let's begin."

Looking at the forty-eight eager, awestruck faces, He smiled and said, "I'm sure you're wondering why you were invited to meet with us. The answer is simple. It's because having never seen Me, you honored Me in your life with your time, talents, love, adoration, praise and worship and laid down your life daily for My sake. And you honored the will of Our Father and surrendered your will by choosing to eat from the tree of life. (Revelation 2:7) Now we want to honor you. Each of you were selected for honor as kings, priests and servants."

Mary, one of the elders and the mother of the Son of Man, bowed before her King, cleared her throat and said, "What my King is saying, is that we want to reward your service on earth with the servant leadership position as king over a nation."

Yeshua looked fondly at His mother and said with laughter, "Mother, you will never change. Always getting straight to the point."

Another elder, taking his cue from the King, added, "As you may have noticed, our King has the weight of the government on His shoulders. (Isaiah 9:6) As the Son of God, He can speak the word and all systems, people, everything can instantly fall into place. But we prefer to engage and do everything through personal relationship with each other, and we're beginning the building process with you."

"We have unlimited opportunities before us," another elder chimed in with excitement. "We have an infrastructure to create, we have an eternity of work to do and we want to begin with you."

Smiling with delight at the enthusiasm filling the room, the Son of Man asked, "Will you join our leadership team as a king and priest over a nation? It's an incredible task. Many of you may feel overwhelmed but I assure you, just as the Holy Spirit guided you previously, He will continue to do so. There is no failure in heaven on earth."

Daniel, one of the elders shared, "We selected you not only for your earthly accomplishments, but for your commitment, loyalty and uncompromising passion to do the will of our King. I served under three different royal administrations, but my only loyalty throughout each was to the One King of kings. If I could do it, so can you."

Another elder, Joseph, son of Jacob, trying to encourage the forty-eight who were still speechless by the magnitude of the occasion, added, "I had no qualifications other than obedience and faith in my King and God when I was elevated into my leadership position, and look how things turned out?"

Addressing the elders, the Son of Man chimed in and said, "Let's not overwhelm our honored friends with our stories." Then leaving His throne, he walked to where the forty-eight were sitting, took a seat among them and asked, "Will you join me in leading this Kingdom?"

Stephen, one of the first martyrs sitting among the forty-eight, replied, "If I may speak for everyone at this table, we all said, 'Yes' before opening the envelope."

Yeshua burst out laughing and replied, "We already knew that. We just wanted to hear you say it."

As He laughed, the room became even brighter. The elders joined in His laughter and the forty-eight broke through their awe and wonder and joined in the laughter as well. When the laughter subsided, the Son of Man said, "Now let's outline the next steps."

# CHAPTER 63

# MODELS & TEMPLATES

In what appeared to be no time, in a period of timelessness, next steps were outlined. Each of the forty-eight selected the nations they chose to lead. Then they agreed on a constitutional plan and custom designed infrastructure that perfectly fitted the uniqueness of each one. They also agreed to mentor successors and rotate positions within designated timeframes. When the high level details were done, the Son of Man strolled back to His throne and declared, "We did it. Thank you. Now we want to honor you as you have honored us."

The elders walked up and stood before two leaders. The King stated, "As you mentor others, so we shall mentor you and we shall continue growing and learning together. Your current mentor is standing before you and in time we shall rotate mentors as well. We will publicly announce and celebrate your appointment later. Today we shall commemorate this occasion with this special crown." He then handed two crowns to each of the elders who placed them on the heads of their mentees, formally introducing them as the king of their designated nation.

When the crown was placed on their heads, the prophet Samuel, one of the elders, stepped aside and poured oil on their heads and said, "We anoint you as kings and priests over the nations." As if rehearsed, the forty-eight removed their crowns, walked to the wooden throne and placed it at the Son of Man's feet. Walking back to the table, they fell prostrate on their faces and worshipped their King.

The elders did the same. Then suddenly the room filled with colorful smoke, lightening, thunder, and the sound as that of roaring lions broke through and said, "This is My Beloved Son, whom I honor and in whom I am well pleased." (Matthew 3:17)

Then the Son of Man, Son of God replied, in the similar booming voice, "This is Our Father, whom I honor, and in whom I am delighted."

Time ceased. When the forty-eight arose from their prostrate position, they were instantly transported back to their new home; to their nation where they were to rule and reign as kings and priests. (Revelation 5:10)

# CHAPTER 64

# COMMUNICATION

The following week, the King of kings made His first Kingdom address to His Bride. Choosing to communicate personally and intimately, spirit to spirit, everyone heard His voice clearly and directly for the first time since their resurrected experience. Wanting to memorialize His message, He sent His written word as well. Everyone received a personally addressed, beautifully embossed envelope bearing His royal red seal with the letter "A" embedded in the center:

*To My Beloved Bride, My Friend,*

*I am so delighted that we are finally united as One, just as the Father and I are One. (John 17:21) As a Bridegroom eagerly waiting for His Bride, I have longed for this day. Having you with Us, is the fulfillment of My destiny. You are the royal heirs, (Romans 8:17) to the Kingdom and as promised, you will receive the inheritance which has been stored up in heaven for you. (1 Peter 1:4).*
*Now that our Kingdom is officially established here on earth, I'm looking*

*forward to ruling and reigning with you as together we take dominion and exercise authority over all that the Father has planned for us. Together we will rebuild, restore and renew our new world. As you can imagine, there is a great deal of work to do, given its current depleted condition. The good news is that we have unlimited time in which to do all that is in our hearts to do.*

*In the meantime, we are delighted to share the formation of forty-eight new nations in our Kingdom, with our new world Headquarters located in Jerusalem. (Revelation 21:21) We have also appointed forty-eight kings to serve you in these nations.*

*Together we will rule and reign, (2 Timothy 2:12) as we rebuild, restore and renew our land. Each head of nation will communicate next steps with you in his/her region. We encourage you to explore your new surroundings, new capabilities and new unlimited possibilities. Just as you exercised faith in Us while on earth, we know that you will continue to do so as you discover the unlimited possibilities that are now yours. And as we have been with you in the past, we will continue to be with you, forever and ever.*

*Even though the veil has been removed and you can see the invisible, prayer shall continue to be our primary communication vehicle. The angels are here to assist and guide you as well. Over the course of time, we will invite each of you to the World Headquarters, where we look forward to meeting you face to face. Holy Spirit will continue to be your guide, and counselor. Remember, nothing is impossible for you as you continue to eat from the tree of life.*

*We will have the first of many Kingdom celebrations shortly. But first, we need to implement an infrastructure where each one of you can play an important role in the administration of our nations. With our leaders guidance, we will need partners in every sphere of life, be it social, administration, judicial, financial, entertainment, science, communication, construction, technical, political, agricultural, educational, industrial, manufacturing, forestry, farming, food preparation, clothing, and all creative arts, etc.* (Conspicuously missing were healthcare, religious, military, mortuary and prison systems, etc.).

*As you already know, our Kingdom is opposite to the prior kingdom on earth. Brotherly love and kindness is our currency; Obedience our goal; Faith our foundation; Prayer our communication; Extravagant giving our treasure; And the written Word of God in the Holy Scriptures is our constitutional guide.*

*Enjoy this temporary rest for now, as we build on a new foundation of mutual trust, love, kindness, mercy, respect, honor, peace, patience, and perseverance. There is much to discover. There is much to do but remember that eternity is before us in the ages to come. We look forward to strengthening our relationship with each other as we continue to grow and develop into the image of Elohim's original design.*

*Again, welcome to the Kingdom of heaven on earth. We have eagerly anticipated this day for some time, and are so delighted that you have chosen us, as we have chosen you.*

*Your Beloved Bridegroom, King and Friend,*
*Son of God, Son of Man,*
*Adonai, Yeshua, Jesus Christ, the Messiah*

Every citizen read the communication as if hearing that familiar voice in their heart once again. Soaring with excitement about what was ahead, they simultaneously bowed in worship, praise and adoration.

# CHAPTER 65

# INFRASTRUCTURE V2

Meeting with their mentors weekly, sometimes daily, the nations' appointed leaders prepared to implement the next phase of their governmental structure. Again consulting the Book of Life, names of potential leaders of states within the countries, cities, towns and villages emerged. Following the same model and using the same selection criteria that was demonstrated to them at the Headquarters, the world leaders selected their next level leadership teams.

With these leaders identified, they developed an infrastructure uniquely suited to their region. Diversity of people, language, culture, thought, and talent was a critical commodity. Theirs was not a one size fits all Kingdom, as reflected by the King Himself. As this phase of the infrastructure took shape, more and more Kingdom Citizens (KC) became engaged, so much so, that eventually every citizen had a vital role to play in the administration of the kingdom, at a local, state and national level. Each one, at every level of administration, was assigned a mentor, always being prepared for rotation or promotion into another role as they desired.

In this timeless realm, the nations within the Kingdom became a hub of activity with zero percent unemployment and one hundred percent contentment. With each kingdom citizen eagerly giving their passionate devotion, talent and resources to advancing the Kingdom and delighting their King, theirs was truly heaven on earth.

It was also the perfect time for their first of many unified celebrations, the public Coronation and Wedding Feast of the King.

# CHAPTER 66

# NOBILITY

Going into His secret place to meet with the Father, Yeshua said, "Abba, we did it. The Kingdom is operational, and we have evidence of the restoration, renewal on the earth as it is in heaven. We're ready. Everything is in place for our first celebration."

Responding with indescribable love and affection, the Father said, "I've been waiting for this day since time began. To see my Son, my only Son, reconciled with His Kingdom, His bride is my delight. Son, you know you have my favor and blessing. Please do as your heart desires. It is my joy to publicly place the crown on your head."

"Father, now that the veil has been removed, I desire that everyone will see Us and be one with Us. Speaking for everyone in the Kingdom, this is our greatest desire and our true cause for celebration. This is what I died for."

"My Son, this has always been Our desire from the foundation of the world. That we would relate with man as One. Just as we walked with Adam and Eve in the cool of the day before sin separated Us."

"This will be Our coronation, Our wedding feast, the consummation of Our relationship, to become One just as We are One," declared the Son of God. (John 17:21)

CHAPTER 67

# THE WEDDING

Mount Zion was the location. Royalty was the theme. The Father designed and created The Crown. The Son of Man, Son of God designed the crowns. The Bridegroom King Himself, directed the preparation and personally delivered each invitation. His Bride prepared her attire.

Everyone in the Kingdom had a vital role in the preparation for this magnificent, once in a life-time, first of many celebrations. Musicians began practicing day and night, creating symphonic melodies in frequencies never before heard. Bakers began designing cakes and other delicious desserts. Chefs were busy creating menus and culinary delights the pallet never before tasted. Farmers became familiar with the perfect, undefiled soil, and began growing pure, delightful fruits and vegetables that titillated the taste buds. Butchers raised healthy animals specifically fit for the King's table. Wineries grew the best grapes ever known to man and created the best wines for the King and His Bride. Florists were enthralled with the choices of colorful, beautiful, fragrant flowers the soil yielded and began creating extravagant bouquets.

Painters, photographers, writers, furniture designers, clothiers, jewelers, and all craftsmen were passionately engaged as they prepared for this significant event.

The Kingdom was a hub of excitement. The time had come. The Father, Holy Spirit, the Son, and His Bride, having seen this day in the spirit, were prepared. The Father, personally attending to His Son's royal attire said, "It was worth it all. I am so proud of You My Son. I have longed for this day to officially present You with Your Bride."

Responding to His Father, the Son said, "Thank You Father. It was all worth it. I would do it all over again, but I'm so glad I don't have to. I never want to be separated from You ever again."

Smiling with unlimited pride as the Father lovingly and tenderly gazed at His Son, He asked, "Are You ready?"

The Son, with the same look in His eyes answered, "With You beside me, I am always ready."

Holy Spirit, observing this exchange, said, "What are we waiting for? Let's do this."

As this exchange was taking place between the Godhead, the Bride was busy ensuring all details were in place and their wedding garment perfect for the event. Likewise, all guests, the angelic hosts, all living creatures, including every animal, bird, fish, tree, flower, even the grass were in pristine array ready to witness this grand event.

In a moment. In the twinkling of an eye. Everyone was transported to Mount Zion. The Bride, standing tall and proud, waiting for her Bridegroom, was stunning in the radiance of the light that illuminated from the Son. Seeing the Bride, a heavenly chorus broke out in song,

"Let us rejoice and exult and give Him the glory, for the marriage of the Lamb has come, and His Bride has made herself ready; it was granted her to clothe herself with fine linen, bright and pure...for the fine linen is the righteous deeds of the saints." (Revelation 19:7-9)

Then a chant rose up from the guests and the Bride, repeating,
"And the Spirit and the Bride say come. And the Spirit and the Bride say come;
And the Spirit and the Bride say come."
(Revelation 22:17)

As they chanted these words, a light, brighter than ever seen in heaven or on earth protruded through the sky. Then fine, mist began spiraling upward and downward. Meeting in the middle, it produced a rainbow like swirl as that of fine water droplets from a gentle fountain dancing in the wind. A sweet smelling fragrance infused the air, releasing gold and silver dust that rested on the Bride. Her skin pulsated at the touch and sparkled with the colors of a perfect sunset. Then a familiar voice broke through and said, "This is my Beloved Son, with whom I am well pleased." (Matthew 3:17)

Out of the mist, the Bride caught first sight of her Bridegroom. It took her breath away. He was arrayed in royal splendor and majesty as none before Him. His features were perfectly chiseled and captivating. His eyes radiated with immeasurable intensity of love as He gazed tenderly at His Bride. Overcome with the full expression of His love, the Bride lowered her gaze, then fell to her knees in praise, worship and adoration.

A hand that was not seen but felt lifted each one to their feet and placed a golden crown on the Bride's head. Even though gentle, the hand was rough, as one having a deep wound with outer scar tissue. The single touch melted her heart. She bowed again in worship and adoration.

In time, the mist cleared. Thrones became visible. The Throne in the middle stood out from the rest in its exquisite beauty. Made of pure gold and inlaid with the finest diamonds, it sparkled with breathtaking brilliance. Upon closer examination, red specks, as that of rubies, glowed from the arm and footrest. The One sitting on the throne, stood and bowed His head. As He did, the swirling rainbow like mist returned. Then a crown appeared hovering over His head. It was the most magnificent, indescribable Crown ever created. It reflected the purest gold, and other precious metals, with the rarest of priceless stones that outlined the Name above all other names, YESHUA. Unseen hands placed it on His head. The gashes the crown of thorns had imprinted on His forehead was covered. It was a perfect fit.

The Voice broke through the mist again and said, "Today, I publicly crown You as King of the heavens and the earth. All power, dominion, authority in the heavens and earth belong to You. It is my delight to present You with your Bride." Then addressing the Bride, the Voice said, "It is also my delight to present you to your Bridegroom, your King."

The sound as that of thousands of shofars broke out and all voices chanted, and danced as

they threw their crowns at His feet and began
singing:

"You are worthy, O Lord
To receive glory and honor and power,
For You created all things
And by Your will they exist and were created."
(Revelation 4:11)

And:
"Worthy is the Lamb who was slain
to receive power and riches and wisdom, and
strength and honor and glory and blessing!"
(Revelation 5:12)

And:
"He who is mighty has done great things for me.
And holy is His name.
And His mercy is on those who fear Him..."
(Luke 1:49)

And:
"No one is holy like the Lord,,
For there is none besides You
Nor is there any rock like our God."
(1 Samuel 2:2)

Then each sang a new song to their
Bridegroom in perfect harmony. When the
singing subsided, a table appeared before them,
laid with all manner of delectable delights of
fruits, vegetables, appetizers, meats, drinks, and
desserts pleasing to all the senses. Everyone ate
and drank to their hearts content with joy and
pure gratification. Without thought of
drunkenness or gluttony, the festivities lasted for
some time. Then it happened. The Bridegroom
took center stage. He extended His nail scarred
hand. The Bride instinctively responded as each

stood, anticipating their first dance. Time faded as the bride and her Bridegroom embraced, face-to-face, heart-to-heart, merging as one, danced to the beat of His heart. Another new song arose:

"Bride born on the Cross
Abiding in His River;
Carried upon the currents of Love
Flowing from the Father and the Son.

Eternal dance of the ages
From beginning to end,
The fusion of creation
the Father's heart for His Son.

Steps choreographed to
the rhythm of
Two hearts beating as One,
The Lamb of God's perfected reflection.

Transformed into His image
the veil has been lifted;
Bride without spot or wrinkle,
Behold, the Bridegroom has come!"
("The Wedding Dance," K. Stockwell, 2020)

The Father looked on with unveiled pride and joy. His Son and His Bride were finally One. Joining His Son in the dance, His swirling rainbow like mist gleefully weaved in and among them as they moved as One. Confessing their love to each other, their first dance was only the beginning.

Continuously learning, growing and developing into His image, the Bride lived and moved and had her being in her Beloved. (Acts 17:28) Soaring to new levels in all spheres of life and doing mighty exploits in the Name of the King, (Daniel 11:32) they explored, discovered and achieved greatness beyond imagination. Each one a vital part of the whole. There was no restlessness. No discontent. No boredom. Now under shared, undefiled, righteous authority and dominion, the earth and those in it, prospered as never before.

The Kingdom of heaven on earth, became the Kingdom of love and the King and His Bride lived happily ever after. (Isaiah 16:5)

# ....THE BEGINNING

# EPILOGUE

"But there are many other things Yeshua did; and if they were all to be recorded, I don't think the whole world could contain the books that would have to be written!" (John 21:25)

"Now to the King eternal, immortal, invisible,
the only God, be honor and glory for ever and
ever." Amen.
(1 Timothy 1:17)

"No eye has seen, no ear has heard
and no one's heart has imagined
all the things that God has prepared for those
who love him."
(1Corinthians 2:9)

"I don't think the sufferings we are going through
now are even worth comparing with the glory that
will be revealed to us in the future."
(Romans 8:18)

"Furthermore, we know that God causes
everything to work together for the good
of those who love God and are called in
accordance with His purpose."
(Romans 8:28)

"Blessed are the meek, for they shall inherit the
earth."
(Matthew 5:5)

"Now to Him who is able to do exceedingly
abundantly above all that we ask or think,
according to the power that works within us, to
Him be glory in the church by Christ Jesus to all
generations, forever and ever. Amen."
(Ephesians 3:20)

"Therefore the Lord will wait, that He may be
gracious to you;
And therefore He will be exalted,
that He may have mercy on You. For the Lord is a
God of justice;
Blessed are all those who wait for Him."

(Isaiah 30:18)

"You prepare a table before me in the presence of
my enemies.
You anoint my head with oil;
My cup runs over.
Surely goodness and mercy shall follow me all the
days of my life;
And I will dwell in the house of the Lord forever"
(Psalm 23:5-6)

"Yours, Lord, is the greatness and the power and
the glory and the majesty and the splendor,
for everything in heaven and earth is Yours.
Yours, Lord, is the kingdom; You are exalted as
head over all.
(1 Chronicles 29:11)

"Do not be afraid, little flock, for your Father has
been pleased to give you the kingdom.
(Luke 12:32)

"The Lord will be King over the whole earth. On
that day there will be one Lord and His Name the
only Name."
(Zechariah 14:9)

"I will give you the keys to the Kingdom of
heaven…"
(Matthew 16:19)

"Blessed are those who are persecuted because of
righteousness, for theirs is the Kingdom of
heaven."
(Matthew 5:10)

"Who is the King of glory?
The Lord, strong and mighty,

The Lord Mighty in battle
…
Who is this King of glory,
The Lord of hosts,
He is the King of glory."
(Psalm 24:8 &10)

# SELAH

# ABOUT THE AUTHOR

*"...But God has chosen the foolish things of the world, to put to shame the wise and God has chosen the weak things of the world to put to shame the things which are mighty; and the base things of the world and the things which are despised God has chosen, and the things which are not, to bring to nothing the things that are, that no flesh should glory in His presence."*
1Corinthians 1:27-29

I have the words "that's me," written next to the above text in my bible. I was born and raised on a small island in the Caribbean until age 14 when I joined my mother in Connecticut. What a culture shock! I'm still recovering from winter.

My journey since then has led me to live in several states on the East Coast, West Coast, and the Midwest. I have a B.S. in Sociology, MS in Human Resources and Business, plenty of real-time, hands-on experience with life, and most importantly, an intimate relationship with Yeshua, my Lord, Jesus Christ. I enjoy writing, reading, gardening, traveling, and spending time with family and friends.

You've heard some of my story. I would love to hear yours. You can reach me at:

a2zredemption@gmail.com
www.a2zredemption.com

# BOOKS BY W. A. VEGA

The Powerful, Thrilling, Mysterious, Suspenseful, Faith-Based, Christian Fiction: **A-Z Redemption** series:
1.      Extraordinary Gifts -Volume 1
2.      A Place Called Hell-O -Volume 2
3.      Incredible Inheritance -Volume 3
4.      The Surrogate's Sons -Volume 4

The Inspiring, Thought Provoking, Meditative, Bible-Based, Christian Fiction: **Beyond Religion** series:

1.      "The Adventures of A. Soul," - Volume 1
2.      "400 Kingdom of Heaven Perspectives," The Adventures of A. Soul, Volume 2
3.      "Through Weak Eyes," The Adventures of A. Soul - Volume 3
4.      "Indescribable," The Adventures of A. Soul, Volume 4
5.      "Incomprehensible," The Adventures of A. Soul, Volume 5
6.      "Inconceivable," The Adventures of A. Soul, Volume 6
7.      "Glorious Intimacy," The Adventures of A. Soul, Volume 7

The Electrifying, Out-of-this-Realm, Parabolic, Christian Fiction: **Beyond Limits Trilogy:** R7:17 TRILOGY – DOMINION, AUTHORITY, PRESENCE
1.      "R7:17 DOMINION," Volume 1
2.      "R7:17 AUTHORITY," Volume 2
3.      "R7:17 PRESENCE," Volume 3

The Captivating, Timeless, Intriguing, Beyond Imagination, Scripture Inspired, Christian Fiction: **Beyond Time Trilogy:**
"R4:14 - NOW," Part 1
"R4:14 - OWN," Part 2
"R4:14 - WON," Part 3


She has also authored:
The Inspiring, Tender, Motivational, Intimate and Personal:
**"MI CARA," - Letters From Heaven, For Such a Time as This"**

www.GlobalPublishGroup.com

Believer Books

BELIEVER BOOKS